Critical acclaim for Peter *Like Us*

"Peter McGehee has a deceptively light touch. *Boys Like Us* pulls us into a world we recognize instantly and travel through effortlessly. The surprise is how well McGehee uses the ordinary details of our daily lives to evoke the demons we all struggle with: sex and love, friendship and family, life and death. I look forward to his next book."
—Helen Eisenbach, author of *Loonglow*

"An utterly delightful book. I enjoyed every word of it!"
— Quentin Crisp

". . . an upbeat, quirky, often humorous and ultimately optimistic book filled with snappy dialogue and colorful eccentrics." — *The Toronto Star*

"The novel takes a mordant, unsentimental view of the AIDS epidemic . . . . a sex-positive novel, a rarity in this age. We are definately not in Jesse Helms' territory."
— *The New York Times Book Review*

"A genuinely delightful comedy so full of tangy dialogue and wacky situations that it screams for the stage, or better yet, the screen." — *Booklist*

". . . a slice of life so deftly spun that there is no question of putting it down. . . . hilarious . . . good comic writing."
—*The Vancouver Province*

". . . an effortless and consistently entertaining read . . . . We need more novels of urban manners this funny. We need more laughter that resonates against the serious issues of our lives." — *Quill & Quire*

"McGehee has the ability, through an invigorating style and witty observations, to transform Zero's everyday life into something we care about. McGehee's intelligence shows through on every page." — *The Boston Guide*

". . . a pleasant, often humorous novel, with fun and imaginative characters . . . . the two chapters in Arkansas could be right out of Steel Magnolias."— *Library Journal*

THE
I.Q. ZOO

PETER McGEHEE

COTEAU BOOKS

Edited by Edna Alford.
Cover illustration and design by Dik Campbell.
Author photograph by Doug Wilson.
Book design by Shelley Sopher.
Typeset by Lines and Letters.
Printed and bound in Canada.

The publisher gratefully acknowledges the financial assistance of the Saskatchewan Arts Board and the Canada Council.

The author gives special thanks to Doug Wilson and Gail van Varseveld who read these stories many times during the writing process and offered encouragement and enthusiasm, and to Edna Alford who rallied for the manuscript at Coteau Books.

The stories or sections of stories have been previously published as follows: "Never Be Famous" in *The James White Review, The Almost Instant Anthology* (Toronto Small Press Book Fair) and under the title "Anon" in *Brushes With Greatness* (Coach House Press); "An Invitation" in *Amethyst* and *Prism International*; "In This Room" in *Amethyst*; "The Art of Coping" in *Grain*; "The Wonderfuls" in *The Toronto Star*; "Survival" in *The James White Review, Stallion, Shadows of Love* (Alyson Publications) and *Canadian Brash* (Coach House Press); "Squirt" in *This Magazine*; "Lunch With Lucille" in *NeWest Review*; "Goldfish" in *Waves, The Toronto Star* and *Scrivener*; "The I.Q. Zoo" in *Grain, Impulse* and *Canadian Brash*; "The Ballad of Hank McCaul" in *Event*; "Sex and Love" in *The James White Review, Canadian Brash* and *The Gay Nineties* (The Crossing Press); "Wilma's Week" in *What Magazine*; "Success" in *What Magazine* and *Canadian Brash*; and "The End of the Season" in *NeWest Review* and *OUT/LOOK*.

Canadian Cataloguing in Publication Data

McGehee, Peter, 1955-
    The I.Q. zoo

    ISBN 1-55050-026-0

I. Title.

PS8575.G454I2 1991   C813/.54   C91-097151-X
PR9199.3.M243I2 1991

C O T E A U   B O O K S
401 – 2206 Dewdney Avenue
Regina, Saskatchewan
S4R 1H3

For Doug

CONTENTS

FEVER AND CHILLS

1. Never Be Famous

Saw your picture in *Newsweek*. In the 'Face of AIDS' issue. The twelve pages of headshots. Selections from the death toll. Month by month.

Your bio said you were in the Peace Corps, that you worked as a lawyer, and with poor kids in the inner city. I don't remember that. It didn't mention your Bisexual Marriage book. It didn't mention "The Donahue Show" or the lecture circuit or the video you made for PBS. I remember that video—the clips of your wedding, the clips of your son who no one talks about, that something's wrong with.

You came to the university as part of our speaker series. I was on the committee and picked you up at the airport. We'd already had Burroughs, Isherwood, and Armistead Maupin, so I was used to people like you, I was ready.

You were into fisting. I'd read that somewhere—*The Gay Sunshine Interviews*, *The Advocate*. You told me about a Crisco party you'd been to the night before. A private party. For married men. Men who played golf, owned houses, and barbecued.

You fell in love with me. Or so you said. You wanted to give me an enema. You were like a little kid about it and made such a scene when I said no. You kept begging. I still said no. You admired my hands. I wouldn't fist you either. No, our love making was nothing out of the ordinary. You were OK. Not great, but OK.

You thought I was talented, wanted to introduce me to Peter Allen or Tommy Tune. If only I'd come visit you in New York.

We exchanged a few postcards, then you sent me your book, inscribed, "For all the good times."

It gave me a rush seeing your picture like that. Someone I know, I said to myself, someone I've slept with, kissed.

And my finger traced a frame around your face. Once.

2. An Invitation

Because of the way he kisses me, his laundered shirts discarded on the chair, starched like he's still in them. Because of the way he sleeps, his back against me in the night. Because of the time we've spent together, feet gently bound by rope.

He never wanted a lover—

Yet these are the wings I clipped.

■

He wakes up coughing. Short of breath. The doctor says: don't worry. Come back in two weeks. We'll do some tests.

My grandmother believed everyone's time was marked, regardless of how you died, the when of it was preordained.

I used to believe that myself. Now I wake up screaming: Fix it!

My crazy aunt just thinks I haven't met the right woman, that one will eventually come along to bring out the man.

You are not a man with a penis in your mouth, up your butt, or in your hand. You are not a man when you dream of steam and the old days when a thousand caressing hands lured you into cubbyholes of flesh. You are not a man when your primary relationship is with an eight-inch piece of rubber and the rest of him you find in a magazine.

Anyone'll tell you passion dies—
But love has a life of it's own.
It's our tenth anniversary next June. Please come.

3. In This Room

Here is the pattern: I sleep only four to five hours. My dreams are hospital dreams, crowded, sick-smelling. They're opportunistic infection dreams, disturbing, what's gonna happen to me and when. All my friends show up, some sick, some well. We laugh and cry about the things we did and the things we never quite got around to.

I wake up suddenly. Thirsty. The city's noisy. Garbage trucks, street cleaners, hookers, the usual thing. I wonder if I ought to take a sleeping pill. I take half.

The dreams turn sexy: a beautiful boy by a swimming pool.

We kiss for the longest time, kisses like water.

He has cream for skin and is void of genitals.

4. Undone

We thought we were safe. We, who had lived through the first years of plague touching no one without protection. We thought we had escaped.

Sure we were haunted. By visions of our younger selves. Tasting the mouths of liberated flesh. Spreading our legs unaware of the poison in our lovers' seed.

Consider the circle of friends that rose from the circle

3

of lust. Such a small world, this heat. Such a cozy, careful weariness. Waiting.

5. There Is Still Some Love in the World

I meet him at my doctor's. He is in the examining room where I am supposed to be, lying on the table with his shirt off. "Sorry," I say. "Didn't know anyone was in here."

"It's OK," he replies. "I'm just waiting for an X-ray." He chokes on the word.

I know all too well what kind of doctoring goes on in this clinic; I know all too well what kind of news he has just received. I leave.

After my appointment, he is waiting for me. No words are exchanged, just a look, and I follow him to his apartment.

He crumples in my arms. Burrows against my chest. Carefully, cautiously, I help him to undress. His skin is like paper covered with stories I have read again and again.

He wants to know if I will hold him until he falls asleep.

Of course. I will do anything.

6. Destiny

I travel to the dead of winter to bury my sadness. To leave it in a motel, by a frozen lake buckled with ice.

The light from the sun illuminates everything but me. I am too dense. Still sad. Still wondering. Still a student of flight.

I have been invaded.

7. Legacy

Between physical illness and this pool of despair, we fly without wings. Through a huge, endless sky: cold, clear, blue, and so generous with time.

We long for our lives to go on and on. For the wings

of death to fall from our backs like charred wood. But we will all rot behind a shower of gold someday.

Stop.

Let me leave a word. A whisper. Something that says: I was here.

Feel the air all around you tingling.

8.   The Art of Coping

My counsellor at the AIDS Committee is undergoing a hair transplant. I am supposed to be talking about my terrible news, but I just keep staring at the little sprouts patched across his forehead, thinking how absurd all this is.

He is my second counsellor. My first one dismissed me. She is very big on hugging. But I have friends to hug, I have my lover. Then when I didn't respond to her battle-over-cancer-story, well, that really cinched it. She pronounced me "blocked." Said I probably had a hatred of women as well. "I do not hate women," I informed her.

"Blah, blah, blah," goes my counsellor, wanting to know if I've decided about the support group.

"I don't think the support group is really for me," I confess.

He is disappointed. I have wasted his time. Nervously, he touches his hair. He does not touch the transplanted part. Perhaps it is too delicate. Perhaps he has forgotten about it. Perhaps it isn't even transplanted yet, but just stuck on for a trial run like they do when you want a sex change. They make you dress and act as the sex you wish to be months before they'll actually alter your genitals. They want to make certain you're serious.

"I don't think you're very serious," says my counsellor.

"I'm very serious," I tell him. "I've joined an activist group. We burned the health minister in effigy yesterday."

The AIDS Committee is on the third floor.

I dance down the staircase like a tap-dancer in an MGM musical.

A musical can reflect the soul.

A musical can defy gravity.
A musical can live forever.

When you die your hair keeps growing.

THE WONDERFULS

I GUESS IT ALL STARTED WHEN THEY MOVED IN NEXT door. Mr. Wonderful was a mortician and opened our first funeral home. Up until then we sent the dead to Billings Creek. "Of all the houses," I kept saying, "why did they have to pick the one next to us?"

"They have to live somewhere," said Mama. She had made them a cake and was icing it.

"That doesn't mean you have to take them anything."

"I'm just being neighborly."

"But he touches dead people. Cuts 'em open and drains their blood."

"Who told you that?"

"It's true!"

"Well, you have to do that to preserve the body. You put a fluid in its place so the dead person looks alive for the funeral. You'll want to look alive for your funeral, I'll bet."

"I'm not having any funeral!" That she could even suggest such a thing, my own mother—

"Everyone dies. It's part of the whole kit and caboodle."

"Not me." I was an American. I'd watched our country shoot a man into space. If we could do that, we could certainly live forever. So I told her.

And she said, "Heaven's where you live forever."

Heaven seemed about as exciting as church. "What if I don't wanta go?"

"Then you go to hell."

Dad was standing at the living room window watching Mrs. Wonderful climb out of her car. She juggled a bag of groceries, a newspaper, and a sack from the liquor store. A cigarette hung from the corner of her mouth. "Damn," she said, kicking the door shut. "Damn!"

Dad had just quit smoking. Once they officially linked it to lung cancer, Mama had put her foot down: he couldn't die until he caught up on his life insurance, and he wasn't about to give those crooks another penny. And there he was staring at Mrs. Wonderful's cigarette.

Mama came through with her cake. "Why's it so quiet in here?"

"Dad was just about to ask me to run down to Smiths' and get him a pack of Newports."

He turned and looked at me. He had no idea I'd even been in the room.

"Honestly," said Mama, "using a child like that. Why don't you just put a gun to your head and save us all the trouble?"

"Quit harpin'."

We watched Mama walk out the door and over to the Wonderfuls'. We watched her speak to Mrs. Wonderful through the screen. We watched her walk back, the cake still in hand.

"What happened?" Dad asked.

"The woman just looked at me, looked at me like I was crazy. Said they didn't eat sweets."

We proceeded to ignore our new neighbors until one morning in June when Mrs. Wonderful appeared at our back door. "We're inviting you over for a barbecue tonight. Six o'clock sharp!" She didn't wait for an answer.

All day we tried to figure out what they wanted. I was

afraid it was to practice their funeral-ing on us. Dad thought they were just trying to butter us up so we'd help 'em clean out their garage or something. Mama said they were just lonesome; "Wouldn't you be? Three months in town and not knowing a soul?" She made a potato salad.

"After what happened last time?"

"Well we can't go empty handed."

"Then we're goin'?"

"Of course we're goin'!"

She combed my hair three times and fussed over my shirttail. We were ready by five-thirty and waited on the back porch for six sharp.

We could see Mrs. Wonderful setting her picnic table. She weighed down the napkins with plastic forks but the wind kept blowing them away. "Damn," she said, not bothering to pick them up. "Damn!"

Mr. Wonderful prepared his barbecue.

"He's a funny-looking man," Mama said.

"Yeah," I told her. "Like he's got a coat hanger stuck between his ears."

He squirted so much lighter fluid on the coals the flame jumped five feet.

"'Nough heat to cremate somebody," said Dad.

"What's cremate?" I asked.

"Never mind," said Mama.

"When you burn something," Dad told me.

"Alive?"

Mama looked at her watch, led us out the back door, and we crossed from our yard into theirs.

I'd been hoping for steak, but would've settled for hamburgers or chicken. I didn't know what to think when Mr. Wonderful started pulling these long, dark, slimy things out of an orange pail and placing them across his grill. Even Dad was alarmed. "What in the name of hell's that?" he asked.

"Eel," Mr. Wonderful answered in a monotone. "Marinated eel."

"Eel?" said Mama.

"It's a fish," replied Mrs. Wonderful. "But if you chew

it right it tastes just like beef. At least where we're from. I guess you don't have it much 'round here."

"No," said Mama, "catfish mostly." She sipped her ice tea. "Just where *are* you from?"

Mrs. Wonderful gestured vaguely toward the napkin-covered hedge. "Oh, out there." She smiled in a strange way. She was a pretty woman. Sexy, even though sexy was a word I didn't know yet.

"I'm allergic to eel," I told her. "Got any hot dogs?"

She looked at me, puzzled.

"Just run over home and get yourself a hot dog," Mama said. "No need to make a scene."

"Get two," said Dad.

That made Mama glare. "Well, I, for one, am willing to try anything. Especially when the Wonderfuls are good enough to cook it for us."

"I'm just normal people with normal ways," Dad muttered, fishing another Bud out of the ice chest.

The heat made the eels' eyes go white. Mr. Wonderful picked them out with a knife and they fell on the coals with a sizzle.

"You follow the baseball?" asked Dad.

"You're talking to a Pirate, Yankee, and Dodgers man."

"All three?"

"Yes sir."

"Well, what do you do when they're playing each other?"

"Win either way." Mr. Wonderful laughed too loudly. He slapped Dad's back. Hard. "What about you?"

"Uh, St. Louis."

I handed over our hot dogs.

"Cremate 'em!" I said, but Mr. Wonderful wouldn't do it. Twice I had to ask him to put mine back on and twice I got my leg kicked under the table. Thanks Mama. But her turn was coming. Soon as they served her that eel.

Eyeless, it hung over the edges of her plate. She watched the Wonderfuls cut into theirs. She tried to imitate them, but the minute she pressed on it with her fork the thing got away from her and went flying into the yard. She had to fight the Wonderfuls' dog to get it back and she lost. I laughed almost as hard as Dad.

Mrs. Wonderful lit a cigarette. She offered the pack around the table. Dad declined, but Mr. Wonderful and Mama both took one. I was shocked. I'd never seen my mother smoke.

By that time the stars had come out. The Wonderfuls pointed to various constellations and said that's what actually determined who we were and what we did in this life. "It's like the tides of the ocean," explained Mr. Wonderful. "The human body *is* two-thirds water." I could just see him draining it out of people after he got through with their blood.

He told us about an anatomy class he'd had in school. He said it was the most beautiful thing in the world, looking into a man or a woman. Lifting away the skin, the heart, the lungs. Studying the muscles. "You wouldn't believe how closely the various parts correlate to something in nature. In the middle of your forehead is a bone the perfect shape of a butterfly." He said it like he was reciting poetry. "That teaches you a respect for the body, beyond the person who inhabits it, which forms the groundwork for what I do today."

All I could say was, "Wow—"

"You know, if you could get your mother to bring you down to the funeral home sometime, I'd be happy to show you around."

"Like on October 31st?" roared Dad.

Mama ground out her cigarette with the toe of her sandal. "That's very kind of you, Mr. Wonderful."

"Call me Otto."

"Otto," she said hesitating. "And I'm sure Tommy would find it most interesting. Once he's old enough to understand." She gave him a look. The conversation went back to baseball.

I decided the Wonderfuls were from another planet. I had a vision in which I saw them peel back their skin, reach inside their chests, and pull out mini TVs. Radios came out of their ears and little cameras out of their eyes. They unscrewed their arms, their legs, and finally their heads which they put in boxes, lined with cotton, like from the jeweler's. That blond head of Mrs. Wonderful's kept staring at me, like it was trying to tell me something, and I was determined to find out what.

I started to spy on them. To record their comings and goings. I even snuck in their house. They didn't lock their back door. So one Saturday afternoon I just walked right in.

I looked in their icebox. I wanted to know what they ate besides eel and found lots of strange juices, powders, and pills, the kind of stuff you'd see years later in health food stores.

I noticed they didn't have a TV in their living room, just a big Magnavox stereo and tons of records. The furniture wasn't like any I'd ever seen. It was all white, uncomfortable, and made you sit up straight.

I crept up the stairs. From the hall I could see the bedroom. The door was halfway shut so I could only see a portion of the bed and Mrs. Wonderful lying on it from the shoulders down. All she had on was a slip and a pair of stockings.

I smelled a cigarette. I figured she'd just woken up from a nap and that I'd better get out of there, but I couldn't move. I was held by some strange magic. I had tingles from my stomach clear down to the middle of my legs.

Dad walked out of the bathroom in his boxer shorts. I was so relieved to see him I wanted to jump up and scream, but the look on his face stopped me. Then I saw it was him smoking, not Mrs. Wonderful, and I said as mean as I could: "I'm gonna tell Mama."

I heard the sound of Mrs. Wonderful's slip as she slid off the bed. I heard her say, "Damn!" And I ran.

Dad caught me within three blocks. I was a crying mess from him chasing me like that.

"We gotta talk," he said, dragging me to his car. He threw me in and slammed the door. He was barefoot.

I was certain he was taking me to the funeral home to get my blood drained. I didn't know what to think when he pulled into the amusement park. He bought two tickets for the Ferris wheel, my favorite ride. We got in the carriage and the one-armed man who ran it threw the switch to make it go.

When Dad asked me what I'd been doing in the Wonderfuls' house, I told him about my vision. He had a good laugh, then said very seriously, "What'd you see in there, Tommy?"

"Nothing," I told him.

He leaned back and put his arm around me. It made the seat rock. We went over the top and my stomach jumped.

"Well," he said, a grin on his face, "I guess both us fellas just had a little something to work out with the Wonderfuls, huh? And there's nothing wrong with that, nothing at all as long as we keep it to ourselves. After all, it's against the law going into somebody's house like you did. Do you understand me?"

I didn't fully. But I said I did, and we shook on it.

The wheel slowed. The man's good arm unlatched the wooden safety bar. I stepped down feeling like I'd grown three feet.

When we got back to the house, Dad took his spot in the living room and turned on the Cardinals. "Sit down and listen with me, son."

I've never been much interested in baseball, but joined him all the same.

Mama came home from the beauty parlor all puffed up and smelling like hairspray. She'd swung by the grocery store and picked up a thick sirloin for Dad to barbecue.

He kissed her real nice.

Mama asked how our Saturday had been. I don't lie good, so I looked out the window. A 'For Sale' sign was stuck in the Wonderfuls' front lawn. "When did that go up?" I asked.

"Been there all week," said Dad.

"I didn't see it."

"Must be blind." He chuckled.

Mama kicked off her shoes and stretched her feet out to touch Dad's.

There we were: a family.

The Eberly's bought the house, but nobody bought the funeral home. Long after the dead got sent back to Billings Creek, people were still talking about the Wonderfuls. The women would say, "I sure wouldn't want to be the one to have to pack and unpack a house that often," and the men would speculate on how much you could make off a funeral in the first place.

But not Mama. She wouldn't say one word. She'd just shake her head like she couldn't believe they ever existed and watch Dad light another Newport with his eye on me.

In their silence I could hear the sound of Mrs. Wonderful's slip. And I'd think to myself: this is how things happen. How the world speeds up.

SURVIVAL

YOU WAKE TO THE SOUND OF TENNIS BALLS. A WINDOW'S open. It's warm. You roll over. You're alone. You wonder where that man is, the movie actor who has you here most Tuesdays. A white sheet trails from the bed. You hear the shower. You see the time. Your money's on the table. You get it and you go.

You drive across the city sipping coffee from a Styrofoam cup. A little V is carved in the plastic top. The trip takes forever. In the hum and screech of the freeway you still hear the tennis balls.

You drive up a hill to this month's home, the pool house behind Barbara and Bill's. You figure you'd better try and sleep, but you can't, so you go out to the pool. Part of your job is to keep it clean. You've grown negligent.

You masturbate in the sun and wish it were midnight. You feel the smoothness of your chest and your scrotum tighten. Your feet point as the feeling gets better, a flexing habit left over from when you danced. You wish something were up your ass. You can almost feel it there. You pinch your left nipple, tickle it.

Someone is watching you. After you come, Barbara appears with a couple of drinks, Bloody Marys for the morning. She says, "Nice, Bruce, nice." You're not a dog, you want to tell her, but you dive into the pool instead. The gleam, the quick chill, and the glide back you up. Surfacing, you reach for your drink and smile.

Barbara's naked except for toenail polish and pool shoes. She slips them off and tests the water with a toe. Inside, her lap dog is throwing himself against the glass doors, barking.

"Helmut, hush," she says, splashing water on her thighs.

You set the drink aside and go back under. You open your eyes. Barbara's legs distort in the ripples like Olive Oyl with elephantiasis.

You float on your back thinking you're thinking of nothing, but you're thinking of a painter you know who's gradually becoming famous. He no longer gives you pictures for free. You like art. You'd like to live in a house full of it, like Barbara and Bill. And you do, sort of.

"What are you thinking?" says Barbara, aiming at you with some of her water.

Slicking back your hair you say, "Nothing."

"Where were you last night?"

"Work."

She smiles. She thinks how precocious you are, how appealing and tantalizing your existence. She'd like to capture you and she's tempted, but then the fun would be gone. She's fifty. She knows how to avoid self-destructive behavior.

You get out, dry off, and walk to a corner of the patio where you can almost see the Hollywood Sign. If you could lean an inch or so further you could see it for sure. As a child, you wanted to be a movie star. You remember that wish, you and a billion others. And you could have done it, but once you realized that, no longer cared. You get by; you live. You're a long way from Amarillo. That makes you smile. So what if you're lazy? Maybe you'll go to New York for the weekend, Fire Island, or even Rome. You need a break, and hell, you can afford it.

Barbara thinks how pretty you are; your white bottom compared to your tan. She watches your weight shift, the muscles along your spine. She considers your legs: lovely, the space between them as you stand there, your soft, succulent masculinity. "Ought to put on your swim-suit, Bruce. It'd be a shame to mess with that line."

You turn toward her, wrapping a towel around your middle. "Ready for your torture?"

"Soon as I finish my drink." The glass rests against her lower lip. She drains it, leaving lipstick on the rim. "Just give me a minute to get on my outfit."

"You're gonna do twice as many sit-ups today."

"Bullshit." She slides open the door. The lap dog runs out in a gust of air conditioning. You throw him into the pool.

"Really Bruce. That isn't very nice."

■

Barbara has on a Jane Fonda outfit and several bracelets. She lies on the thick carpet of her dressing room. You sit with your legs in second position, leaning forward on your elbows.

"I hate having to exercise," she tells you.

"The sooner you start, the sooner we finish."

She stretches. She's feeling very matter-of-fact. "Do you love my husband?"

"No."

"Neither do I. I used to, but it didn't last. Not that it's supposed to."

"Lunge left eight times, be sure the knee goes over the foot."

She does so. "I don't know how you sit like that. It'd kill me."

"Flat back, now plié."

"This sudden fascination Bill has developed for young men is an absolute mystery to me."

"Stomach in, arms out, shoulders down, and circle."

17

"He's never showed signs of homosexuality before, and he is over sixty."

You correct her posture.

"God this hurts."

"Then don't do it. It's for you, not me."

"I hate that attitude from a teacher."

"Eight more." You count them out loud to make her feel better.

"Actually, just between you and me, I've never found Bill a very sexual person. He works too hard. Not that there hasn't been the odd time, even the odd affair on both our parts."

"Keep your hips straight. Face front."

She looks at you from the awkward position of a side stretch thinking she deserves more of a response than that. You agree. "I don't think he's very sexual either."

She stands upright. "What do you do, the two of you?"

"He likes to watch me masturbate."

She's won. "So do I."

A plane flies too low, making outrageous noise, shaking the house. "That's not supposed to happen in this neighbourhood," she informs you.

"Sixty-four sit-ups, then we're done."

You feel paralyzed. You feel like everything you're half good at has been done a thousand times. You scold yourself for your lack of imagination and discipline. You resent belonging to a crowded generation. You resent the competition. You look at a crowd of people and see a billion single cells, each self-encased and self-sufficient. You're immobilized. Lucky you were born beautiful. Lucky to carry it off. That's the one thing you do well. Though it's work, it's an effortless kind of work. A talent, you decide.

■

"Rosita will fix you lunch when you're ready, Bruce. A nice salad? I've got my card game." She looks at you funny. "Are you on drugs?" She throws her car keys in the air and catches them on the jingle. This is her cheerio gesture.

You go back to the pool. When Rosita brings your lunch tray you say, "Gracias."

She tells you, "Speak English to me, please."

■

You've got on your swimsuit. You put the air mattress in the pool and slide on top of it. You think about taking a nap in the sun. You smoke a joint. You think how peaceful this part of the afternoon can be, so quiet, everyone gone.

You're stoned and daydream Sidney Ng, the day you met at the beach. There he was, a Vietnamese midget strolling the boardwalk in a top hat, tails, and carrying a cane. You thought you were hallucinating. He said "hello" with an effort against an accent. He told you he was in business, the funeral business, and you laughed.

"But I have great admiration for the American style with death," he assured you.

"Is that why you're in that get-up?"

"Please, what is wrong with my costume?"

You need to pee. No one's looking. You think about peeing in the pool. You've always done that and the act itself is like a safe memory. You wonder if anyone else pees in this pool, Barbara or Bill. The thought that they might disgusts you.

Your cock burns as the urine passes. Shit. You try to forget about it, but can't. Your doctor's trained you well. You get out of the pool and pick up the pool phone. Rosita's talking to someone in a speedy Spanish. You hang up. A few minutes later she's off. You call directory assistance and ask for the number. You dial. Your doctor is expensive but you get an appointment for that afternoon. You bathe, masturbate, then dress.

■

The doctor's office is empty except for a homely male receptionist and one other patient. You check in. Your chart's already pulled.

The other patient looks at you cruisy. You like it until

you think he's looked a little too long, too hungry you decide, and you pick up a magazine. *The Advocate.* The headline has to do with AIDS. You put it back down. You pick up the newspaper. Reagan is visiting a Nazi cemetery, wants more money for the contras, and is finally negotiating a date to negotiate with the Russians. You turn the page. "26,000 Blacks at South African Funeral. Does America Have a Stake in Apartheid?" You put that down too. You pick it back up to see what section the movies are in. The section you're looking for isn't there. You pick up a *McCall's* with two articles that interest you, one on Karen Ann Quinlan and one on Mary Tyler Moore. The other patient smirks at your choice, and when he realizes you've seen him do it, genuinely smiles. You genuinely smile back. The receptionist calls you in.

As your doctor examines you, he tells you about someone he knows who's casting a TV movie. He tells you this every time you visit. "And it just so happens they need a tall, dark, handsome type with ice-blue eyes. Interested?"

"Sure, Doc."

"You really ought to be in the business, kid."

"I am."

You both laugh. He pats you on the ass like a father and tells you to do up your pants. He looks at a slide under a microscope. "Nongonococcal," he announces, and hands you medication from a metal drawer. "Stay out of the sun and no drinking."

■

You drive mindlessly through Santa Monica. You see a travel agency and park. You tell the woman in there you'd like to go someplace, someplace not too sunny, someplace in the rainy season. She suggests the Brazilian rain forest but you've already been there.

"Well, that's about the only place I can guarantee rain." She offers you a Marlboro. You take it. You only smoke when you're about to spend a lot of money, which excites you, and the cigarette calms you down. She flicks her lighter, controlling the flame flirtatiously.

"I'd like to go someplace with a primitive culture." You surprise yourself.

She suggests a tour of Indonesia. "And they always have some rain," she adds.

"Not a tour. Just one place."

She shows you a pamphlet. You look at the map part, then the hotels, then the pictures. You pick the place with the least information. "New Guinea."

She's taken aback. "I haven't any references in New Guinea."

"Just the ticket. That's all I want."

She seems put out, then remembers her commission. "First Class or Coach?"

"First."

"When would you like to leave?"

"Today."

She looks something up. "How long do you plan to stay?"

"I don't know."

"You can get a visa on arrival if it's less than thirty days."

"Twenty-nine then."

"You'll need malaria pills. Oops, today's flight left at two."

"Then book it for tomorrow."

She fiddles with the ticket computer. "Qantas via Sydney. You can have a stopover if you like, it's included in the price."

"No thanks."

"Cash or charge?"

"Charge." You hand her Bill's card.

You go back to your doctor's. The homely receptionist says, "Forget something?"

"Malaria pills. I'm going to New Guinea."

■

That evening after cocktails, Bill visits you in the pool house. He stands with his lips an inch away from yours.

21

His mouth is open and you are asked to simply stand there and breathe. He's Dr. Frankenstein. This ritual will eventually transfer him into your body and you into his.

He undresses you like a fragile doll. Your skin is so silky it frightens him. He tries not to touch it. You sprawl on the bed, touch yourself, and begin. There's no feeling. He asks what's the matter. You tell him you don't know, but you have an infection.

"Good god," he says. "I thought you knew how to take care of yourself." He picks up his drink and leaves.

You're nauseous from the antibiotics and take a nap. You wake in time to have supper with Barbara by the pool. Bill is elsewhere. The silver makes an eerie sound, hitting the plate, cutting the food. The ice in the scotch glass cracks. The sky is orange and heavy with smog. Barbara turns on the pool lights, remote control.

"Bill tells me you have an infection."

"It's nothing really."

Dinner finishes. You ask for a joint. She gives you one of her best. You smoke. The silence is accompanied by nothing unusual, just a regular night. You sit still, stoned. You decide you like Barbara and smile. She smiles too. Your smiles are the smiles of children and the moment is sweet. You try to hold it but the shuffling of dishes makes it die.

You rise, take off your pants for the pool, and walk to the lighted edge. You stand there, the night air around you, lost in thoughts unknown. You grip the concrete subconsciously with your feet, then pierce the water, splashless.

SQUIRT

PEGGYLEEN DOESN'T WANT ME TO GO IN THERE WITH her. She says she wants to have her abortion alone. OK, I say, fine, go ahead. So I'm waiting in the car. I climb over the stick shift to the driver's seat and put my hands on the wheel. I'm gonna drive home. That's why she brought me.

I watch the fringe on her leather jacket swing as she walks into the Doctor's Building annex. The annex is made of concrete blocks and looks like a bank branch. She's at the reception counter, bulletproof glass between her and the appointment lady. Someone threw a bomb last Easter so they can't be too careful. Peggyleen announces her name into a microphone. After the lady looks her up on the appointment sheet, she buzzes her into the waiting room.

They won't bother to counsel her much. Since it's her second, she's already heard their spiel. They'll try to give her the Pill though and she'll accept, to be polite, but she won't actually take them. She says they make her too fat and she's already heavy enough on account of her boobs.

People call her Dolly Parton II. Mom says they're just jealous.

Mom takes up for Peggyleen. With me, she keeps her distance. I remind Mom of everything she can't understand. Not that we fight exactly, there's just been a sort of withdrawal, like we're already finished with each other. If she were my real mom she wouldn't do that. She thinks she's lost me, is what she says. The problem is I tell her the truth. Peggyleen tells her exactly what she wants to hear. Gossip mostly. Peggyleen makes her laugh until she doubles over in a coughing fit. But Mom doesn't even know Peggyleen. The main thing about Peggyleen is loyalty. When you tell her something, she listens.

A red station wagon pulls up to the stoplight. My insides turn to ribbons. I think of Mom going off on her rampage and Uncle Ray beatin' me with his fishing pole. I look back at the station wagon. It's just a woman with some kids. I wonder what Peggyleen's kid would've looked like.

Peggyleen's last abortion took about an hour and a half. I was in the car then too, only I didn't have my Learner's Permit, so couldn't drive her home.

I'm bored out of my mind. I can't turn on the radio 'cause of the battery, so I try doing some homework. I'm reading *Huck Finn* for English, but it's such a boring book my mind keeps going back to Peggyleen.

It's Tom Ed who's the father. Well, not really the father since there's not gonna be any baby, but it was Tom Ed's penis that gave the seed.

I can't imagine them actually doing it. Peggyleen says you can never imagine it until you've done it, then you can't think of nothing but. What she keeps forgetting is I've done it.

I think of how it'd feel to have a baby in your body and that I can really imagine, because if there's one thing I know for sure it's my body. Why else do you think Hank McCaul got run out of town? It wasn't what everyone said. I knew what I was doing. I'd been getting in his car since I was twelve and he didn't make me do anything I didn't want to. Only mistake I made was telling Mom.

I look back at the stoplight. I've gotta learn how to lie.

I'm just twiddling my thumbs in this town, ticking away like a time bomb. But I'll get out. It's Peggyleen that worries me. She'll end up just like Mom: marrying somebody, having kids, divorcing, taking some job she hates. 'Course, Peggyleen says you can end up like that anywhere, and I guess she's got a point.

I think of how Dad used to clip his toenails into Mom's slippers, how mad she'd get, and how hard he'd laugh. She says he laughed her right out of loving him.

I look over at the clinic.

I see Mark Baber about to cross University. I'm so bored I forget I don't want anyone to see me in the parking lot and honk. Mark looks up, waves, and walks over. I don't want to seem too anxious, just sitting there, so I start rubbing Peggyleen's cigarette ashes into the carpet.

"I'm goin' over to the mall," Mark says. "Wanta come?"

I look at my watch. It's only been ten minutes. "Sure."

I lock up Peggyleen's car. Mark and I walk through the parking lot. I get this weird feeling I'm expanding like some kind of Gumby doll. I'm close to twenty feet tall. We jump over the guard rail. I see a distorted image of myself in the metal and wonder if Peggyleen's kid wouldn't've looked just a little bit like me, which is crazy.

The mall's got up a sign that says, "No Mall Walkers." Mall walkers scare off shoppers. We bought Mom a pair of Nikes last Mother's Day so she could mall walk, but she smokes too much to walk unless it's to get somewhere. Coughing's her exercise. She coughs her way out of bed in the morning, coughs her way through her first cup of coffee, and coughs her way through her first cigarette. Then she takes our dog, Rebel, out to the elevator. She's taught him how to walk himself. She just puts him in and punches L. Rebel rides down to the lobby solo and waits by the front door until someone comes along to open it.

Mark says, "Missed you at the show last Saturday."

"Didn't have the money." My first lie. I was with red station wagon. Met him hitchhiking. I could be in love if I wanted to be and that's all I'm sayin'.

"How's Peggyleen?"

"Fine." See the doctor smile? See him set her feet in the stirrups? Just like having your innards vacuumed, is how she puts it. Good thing she's only eight weeks.

"Ever do anything with her?"

I just look at Mark.

"You could, you know. It wouldn't be incest. Not really."

I look right at his neck and think how Peggyleen says the best birth control is to choke a guy's dick. Just when he's about to come, to squeeze so hard nothing can squirt out.

I'm still looking at Mark's neck when he says, "Let's go down to Penney's and check out the bikes." I hate that store. The whole place stinks from the candy counter. Even the underwear that's sealed in plastic.

We pass a cake contest in honor of the Sesquicentennial. A lady from the Junior League invites us to vote. I vote for the one of the Arkansas flag. Not because I'm patriotic or anything, but because it's the best. In fact I vote for it twice. Once going into Penney's and once coming out.

Mark sees Carol Ann Fullbright. He steers us right toward her but says, "Act like we don't see her. Don't say anything until she says something first."

Carol Ann says, "Hi."

I say "Hi" back, but Mark plays coy.

Finally he says, "Decided about Sunday night?"

"You mean Youth Group?"

"You gonna go with me or not?"

"I don't know. You'll have to call and ask."

"I'm asking now."

"'S not the same." Carol Ann flips her hair. It's long and blond. "Seen Shari anywhere? I'm s'posed to meet her."

Mark looks down toward Moses Record Store. "Come

on, Bobby, let's go see if they've got that new 'Power of Love' in."

We're looking through the Top 40. Carol Ann and Shari are looking through the classical. They take band. Carol Ann plays flute and Shari plays the saxophone. Carol Ann stage whispers to Shari something about Sunday night. Mark, flipping through the records, says, "All ya gotta do is say yes or no."

Carol Ann grabs Shari by the hand and leads her back into the mall, giggling.

"Damn," says Mark. Then he practically yells, "Guess I'll just have to take Shannon."

Carol Ann stops, turns around, glares, then stomps off.

"Well Bobby, guess there's nothing else for us to do but go get a goddamn Coke."

We go to Frankie's. Mark buys. Not that I'm broke, it's just that we sometimes trade off. We've known each other a long time. He used to live upstairs from us until his mom remarried and moved 'em out to a house.

When Mom and Dad started having their trouble, Peggyleen and I used to stay over at their place. Mark and I used to be best friends, inseparable, two versions of the same thing.

We sit by the window and watch the shoppers. I bite the end off my straw and dig the ragged part into my gums. They bleed but it doesn't hurt. I imitate Dracula.

Mark says, "Gross."

I bite on some ice and wonder how bad Peggyleen'll bleed. Last time it went on over a week and she scrubbed the toilet like a maniac every time she went to the bathroom hoping Mom wouldn't catch on. But it could've just been her period.

Peggyleen'd kill me if she knew I'd left her car unattended. She's nuts for that stupid car. First thing she does in the morning is look down in the parking lot to make sure nobody's stolen it. Like it was something to steal. Only reason she thinks it is is 'cause she bought it with her own money. Dad was real proud when he heard about her saving up enough. He sent her a smiley-face deodorizer thing to hang from the mirror. But Peggyleen hates things like that. She gave it to Mom's boyfriend, Crow, to sell at one of his yard sales. Crow got himself all deranged in Vietnam and doesn't have to work. He just drinks a lot and makes a fool out of Mom. Mom acts like she's Peggyleen's age, Crow falling all over her, falling all over Rebel. I ask her why she puts up with him. Depends on the day to hear her tell it. Sometimes it's 'cause he's sexy and other times she just picks at the mole on her face.

Crow was over last night hitting Mom up again for some of her pay. "A loan," he calls it. She only gives him half of what he asks for, which he's finally figured out, so he was asking for twice as much. He even brought a hand-carved coffee table as collateral. She said that wasn't gonna change a thing, that it looked like something some hillbilly carved. "Wasn't no hillbilly," he said. "Was my own goddamn grandfather."

I was in Peggyleen's room. She had her hair rolled up on little orange juice cans and was fiddling with the radio trying to get a song to show me some new dance step. Then we heard the television smash into the living room wall. Peggyleen fastened her robe, went in, and told Crow it was time to go.

'Course Mom was cryin' real hard 'cause she loves TV more than anything—games show, soap operas, sitcoms—you name it. Peggyleen held her from one side and I held her from the other. Mom still had on her beauty parlor uniform, still had hair clips up and down her lapel. They were gray and gooey from newsprint and hairspray, and jabbed in our faces as we hugged.

And this is how it always is: a big blow out, then back to the angel stage. Her good humor will last until one thing too many goes against her, then the whole thing'll keep building until she loses herself another TV.

Mom looked in her checkbook to see if she had enough to get a new one. She didn't. She had me and Peggyleen help her throw the coffee table down the garbage chute.

I point over to Frankie's cafeteria line. "Think they got any openings?"

"I don't know. Ask."

I go up to the counter and get a job application from the assistant manager. I don't fill it in as carefully as I did the cake ballots.

Mark watches me lie about my age and waits to see if I'll really hand it in. I do. The assistant manager glances it over, then puts it in a drawer under the cash register. "We'll call if anything comes up."

Mark sees Carol Ann and Shari. He runs out and asks 'em if they wanta go down in the parking garage. Carol Ann looks at Shari, Shari looks at Carol Ann, then Carol Ann says, "Sure."

We find us an unlocked LTD.

Mark and Carol Ann take the back seat and immediately start making out. I get in behind the wheel. I roll down the window and lean my head out. Shari and I talk about school and I feel dumb because I'm not even trying to make out with her. I'm thinking about Peggyleen and that damn vacuum, how weird that must feel, and how boring all this is.

Shari tells me she got a *D* in Science. I tell her, "All you gotta do's pin a bunch of bugs to a piece of Styrofoam—"

Mark and Carol Ann come up for air. Carol Ann's got an embarrassed expression on her face like Mark's brushed against her with a boner. I've got one too, though Shari and I haven't even touched.

I look at my watch. The whole thing's probably over by now. Peggyleen's probably in the recovery room drinking a glass of orange juice like they give you after you've given blood. Maybe she's looking out at the car wondering where I am.

I lay a kiss on Shari. She's got OK lips, but she's too nervous about it. Mark smiles. I tell him I've gotta go. We get out of the LTD and head back through the mall.

Mark says he'll walk me as far as University. "Don't forget about Youth Group," he says to Carol Ann. Shari looks at me like why don't I ask her?

Carol Ann says, "Call, Mark!" and giggles. She elbows Shari to giggle too.

Mark and I push through a bunch of senior citizens who've shown up to protest the "No Mall Walkers" rule. They have signs that say, "We Need Our Exercise!"

At the bottom of University Hill, Mark and I say good-bye. He looks at me. "Good to see ya," he says and smiles. I smile back.

I sit in the car drawing X's in the dusty dashboard. Finally, Peggyleen comes out.

"Ain't nothing fun about that," she says. "Only thing I can say is it's over. Goodbye Tom Ed."

I start the car, drive out of the parking lot and onto University.

"Problem with him is his dick's too fat. No amount of choking's gonna stop his little fuckers."

"Did he pay you for it?"

"Are you kidding? Think I'd even tell him? I'd be ruined for sure then!"

She pulls down the sun visor. She looks at her face in the mirror. "God, I'm white. What do you say we go over to the tanning salon? Tammy's working and she can get us in for free."

We sit at the University and Markam stoplight waiting to turn left. I'm cautious. I sit through it twice. Peggyleen tells me to go the minute it turns red.

"Yeah, and wreck your car?"

"You ain't gonna wreck my car." She leans down and pushes the gas pedal with her hand. We lurch out into the intersection. "Go!" she hollers. "Gun her, Bobby!" She laughs her crazy laugh, spastic cackles and great gulps of air.

I pull into the parking lot about to have a heart attack. I drive around to the entrance by the tanning salon.

"What did they do with it?" I ask.

"With what?"

"The baby."

"It's not a baby, for christsake. It's just a little blob no bigger than this." She points to her thumbnail.

"They still gotta do something with it."

"They throw it away."

"I would've kept it for you."

"You don't know what you're talking about, Bobby. Kids never turn out like you think. Look at us." She opens her door. "You coming or not?"

"No."

She reaches in her purse and pulls out a couple of bucks. "Then go get yourself something to eat."

I go back to Frankie's. I order a cheeseburger and ask the assistant manager if I've gotten the job yet.

"Like I said, we'll call."

"The cheeseburger's to go," I tell him.

I head through the mall to the back exit. I pass a Ralph Lauren display in M.M. Cohn's big window, giant pictures of men and boys in a ranch setting. I look at one man with slicked-back hair and a lasso. Then I see my own image superimposed on his, my cheap clothes and stupid face.

I climb the hill behind the parking lot and sit up on the guard rail. I unwrap the cheeseburger, smelling the combination of onions, pickles, and ketchup. The grease oozes out of the bun, gurgling like something live, slowly suffocating.

I eat, watching the cars and rigs barrel through town on the freeway heading who knows where. I see myself in one not looking back.

When Peggyleen comes out of the tanning salon, she sees me sitting up there and hollers, "Come on, Squirt."

I run down the embankment and through the parking lot, dodging cars. I'm out of breath when I get there, giddy. I hug her. She looks at me oddly, puts on her sunglasses, and climbs into the driver's seat.

"Thought you wanted me to," I say.

"Changed my mind, Bobby. Get in."

LUNCH WITH LUCILLE

LUCILLE DROVE ZIPPY TO THE VET TRYING TO MAKE ONE last deal with God. If He would just let the dog live, she'd promise never to bore anybody with her divorce again. In fact, if she could keep the whippet, she'd forget Stanley ever existed.

She almost had a wreck. She swerved back onto the road knowing it was no good. Zippy had to be put down. And she accepted it, though there was a part of her that still hoped.

The fingers of her free hand traced the length of the dashboard. The inside of the car was one of the few familiar things left. So much else had changed: the children, the divorce, the loss of the house, all the weight she'd gained.

Lucille had believed in God since she was a little girl. It's not that she expected chariots. She just felt if she did her part, He ought to do his.

She wished she had a cigarette, or a card game to go to, or someone to commit adultery with, but onward she drove with Zippy by her side.

Lucille loved driving. The act itself worked wonders.

She remembered the night she realized Stanley was having an affair. She waited until dawn for him to come home. Finally, she called her new friend Charlotte. She'd met her at a Symphony fundraiser and Charlotte had been kind. People seldom took to Lucille that way.

Lucille let the number ring and ring. When Stanley finally answered she was confused. "Charlotte?" she said, full of hesitation. Then the whole scenario fell painfully into place. She dropped the receiver and loaded Zippy into the car. She drove to the Crowchild Trail and circled Calgary four times before she felt calm enough to return home.

The time Lucille's mother died she drove all the way to California and back. The summer her daughter announced her lesbianism, Lucille took on the Northwest Territories. "Remember that, Zippy?" No reply.

Poor Zip. She'd lost a leg to cancer, suffered cataracts, diabetes, and had even had a heart by-pass. Now she was in a coma. That began last Christmas Day. Lucille was still living in the family house. She'd thought to enjoy the festivities in the company of her beloved canine and forget all the people no longer there. She descended the grand staircase lined with her family portraits. She had a breakfast of Bloody Caesars. She even allowed Zip a nip.

The dog seemed fine. Mind you, she wasn't what you could call spry, but for her condition, she seemed almost chipper. She licked Lucille's knees as she did every morning. The dog and the woman were in perfect harmony.

Zippy ate a little breakfast, then curled up in front of the couch. When she didn't wake for lunch, Lucille panicked. She wasted no time getting Zippy to Emergency. After a considerable bribe, the doctor on duty agreed to examine her, hooked her brain up to a computer, and confirmed her to be a vegetable. He said she ought to be taken to a proper vet and put to sleep.

"But if she's a vegetable, she can't be feeling pain. Why shouldn't I keep her?"

"You'd have to watch her around the clock."

"I already do. It's my pleasure."

"But think of the expenses. You could feed a starving nation on what it'd cost."

"I don't care. She's my friend!"

By nightfall, Lucille had installed a mini-hospital at the foot of her bed. Things admittedly became more difficult once she was forced out of the house. Behind her back Stanley donated it to the province. The Alberta Historical Society had it renovated and opened to tourists. Lucille was moved to a cramped penthouse. It wasn't that she minded so much until she discovered her paintings, furniture, and even wardrobe were to stay behind with the house. All she managed to get away with was a mink cape, her car, and Zip.

The dog's coma haunted her terribly. She went so far as to make an appointment with the woman psychiatrist she had seen during menopause. The doctor suggested the dog's illnesses were invented by Lucille as a means to further control her ex-husband. Lucille was so wounded by this realization that she went perfectly berserk. "Why you pompous bitch!" she said, slapping the doctor across the face. The doctor hollered for help. It took three orderlies to subdue her. And what was that drug they had injected her with? How pleasant it had been! If only she could get it now when she needed it most.

But the doctor was right. Her divorce wouldn't be technically final until the death of the dog. That had been the sole term to which Lucille had clung during her year in and out of court.

Lucille had been rich when she married Stanley. Stanley took control of her money and lost it all. When her parents died and she inherited theirs, he tricked her into more investments.

During the divorce her sense fell apart. In trying not to think about it she became obsessed with the oddest things. She drove to the cattle show down at the Stampede and tried desperately to buy herself the title of "Shorthorn Lassie." A week later she was arrested in the Bay for shoplifting baby clothes. She offered no explanation. It had been years since she'd known a child. She lurked around school yards and exposed herself to little boys. She wore only her cape and a nylon stocking pulled over her head.

She was eventually declared a legal lunatic. The court gave her thirty-six hours to secure someone to look after her interests. If she failed, she would be institutionalized.

She tried her son. As usual, he wouldn't take her call.

She called her daughter. Susan's lover answered.

"This is Lucille Larson. Is Susan still living at this number?"

"Suz?" Dora bellowed. "It's for you."

Susan picked up the phone. Lucille was overcome with emotion. "Baby!"

"Mom, I'm not a baby."

"Susan, then—"

"What do you want?"

"This isn't easy for me to say, but I need you."

"You don't need me. You need who I used to be. You can't accept me as I am."

"I accept you! Baby, please."

"For the last time, I'm not a baby! It's high time you learned to deal with your own problems. Goodbye!"

Lucille stared listlessly at the dead receiver until a recording came on and told her to hang up.

That left Stanley. And he was only too willing to further his control on her welfare.

The court gave him everything. Stanley put Lucille on an allowance. His latest line was to eventually adopt her. He had a theory he could spend even less on her if she were legally his daughter. He planned to install her on the third floor of his new home along with his illegitimate son.

Lucille pulled into the vet's parking lot. She turned off the car. She hoped she didn't look too drunk. Again, she thought of God.

She picked up the sleeping Zippy, portable life support system and all. The dog was down to eleven pounds. The main problem with carrying her was her legs. They flopped willy-nilly, suffered twitching spells, and sometimes kicked out violently. The first time that had happened was in a supermarket. Zippy knocked down a shelf full of Grape Nuts. Lucille fainted, thinking her faithful companion was finally coming to. Then the store manager threw a glass of cold water in her face. A policeman wrote her a ticket for bringing a dog into the store to begin with. That's when Lucille suggested the vet just lop off Zippy's remaining legs. She didn't see what good they were doing her. They no longer served their natural purpose and it would make her so much easier to carry.

The vet laughed. "What you ought to do is put her out of her misery."

"But she's not miserable!"

"We all fear loneliness, Lucille."

"I don't. Not as long as I have my dog!"

She opened the door to the clinic. She knew it was a monumental step. She contemplated the freedom beyond such devastating loss. She wondered if she wouldn't do something great. The thought was just about to make her feel better, but the sadness hit her first. She stood inside the waiting room, in the path of the air conditioner, frozen, with the dog in her arms.

She felt Zippy's heartbeat. She felt her ears. The shape of her sweet head. The snout. Neck. The tautness of her hide, even now at the age of sixteen.

She remembered the day she had first met Zippy. She was living in Houston at the time. Stanley had been transferred to head office. She'd gone to the dog races with her cleaning lady. Zippy won Grand Prize. Lucille attended every subsequent race the dog ran. When they retired her, Lucille would have paid any price for the honor of giving the champion a home. Zippy's owner only wanted a token dollar. With the money she saved, Lucille commissioned a diamond collar. The day she picked it up, she wept. It was perfectly gorgeous, so much more appropriate than the rhinestones most dogs wear.

"So we're finally gonna do it?" said the receptionist.

"I have an appointment with the doctor."

"Yes, he's expecting you. Go on in. Goodbye, Zippy."

Lucille waited in the examining room a good five minutes before Dr. Collis appeared. His voice had a desperate edge. She recalled the day he grabbed her bosom, and got out her emery board. The dog was on the table. The doctor drew a syringe, then asked if there were any last words.

"Just get it over with," she said, filing.

Zippy's body seemed to melt with relief as the lethal serum did its trick. The emery board stopped. Lucille's throat felt dry. She swallowed.

"That's all there is to it." The doctor covered the dog's corpse.

"I'd like to keep her collar," Lucille said, which irritated the doctor. He had thought how nice it would've looked on his wife.

"Will you take it off her for me?" asked Lucille.

"What's the matter? Afraid she'll bite?"

"She was my friend," Lucille said quietly.

The vet granted her this small kindness. "Think of her in heaven."

"I wish I believed in such a place. The man from the pet cemetery will be by for the body. Thank you for all you've done."

"That's OK. You'll get my bill."

Lucille walked solemnly to her car. Once safely inside, she let herself cry. She cried so hard she could barely see to drive. She thought she'd have a wreck, maybe even kill herself, but she didn't care enough to be careful.

She drove to a nearby 7-Eleven. She bought a box of candy and a giant-sized Coke. She caught her reflection in the glass doors as she pushed her way out. Her hair looked like a fright wig. She tried to pat it down.

Tottering across the parking lot, she considered her options: she could put a gun to her head, or she could just keep driving.

She got in the car and ate a piece of chocolate.

The tank was full.

What the hell.

GOLDFISH

GOLDFISH DIED ON A MONDAY. I REMEMBER IT WAS A Monday because Monday was the day the maid came to clean. She vacuumed runways into the living room carpet. It was a runway I followed to the fish bowl.

Goldfish had been sick for a week and was floating upside down. I poked at him with a finger. Dead.

He had been a present from grandmother Alice, a sort of consolation prize on account of her having to stay in bed all the time nursing her cancer. No more accompanying me to the park or eating out at the Magnolia Cafeteria where the menu, like the organist, never changed.

I put Goldfish in a jewelry box coffin and presented him to my mother. She was frantically frying lamb chops, which were expensive, but Alice's favorite. "Get that fish out of here!" she hollered. Then just as quickly, she changed her mind. She picked Goldfish up, held him between two well-polished nails, flicked on the disposal, and threw him down.

Fish scales splattered out. "What'd you do that for?"

"He was dead."

"Is that what you'll do to Alice?"

"Alice won't fit down a disposal."

"She would if you chopped her up."

■

"Alice, did you hear about Goldfish?"

"No darlin', what?"

"Dead."

"We'll get you another fish."

"I don't want one."

"Well we'll get one anyway."

On her bedside table was an empty syringe. "Can I have it?"

"You may."

I sold them as water guns and had a cigar box full of money from the project. I jumped on her bed. She winced.

"You're not as much fun as you used to be," I said.

"Want me to read you a story?"

"No."

"Not even *The Hats of Bartholemew Cubbins*?"

"You mean *The Five Hundred Hats of Bartholemew Cubbins*. No."

She looked out the window, then swung her legs to the floor. One was huge, the other was skin and bones. She positioned her walker. She smelled. "Help me to the bathroom."

"It'll cost you."

"How much?"

"Dime."

"Well, you can get it out of my pocket book when we get back."

She shuffled across the hall. I stood guard while she hiked up her gown then landed on the toilet seat with an uncontrollable plop.

■

In the next neighborhood over was a vacant lot. Our yardman, Figaro, had a shed there. Figaro told fantastic stories about being an exiled king from some tropical island. Said he swam all the way to Little Rock by way of New Orleans, up the Mississippi River to the Arkansas, then halfway across the state. He claimed he could fix anything. I'd seen him fix record players, bicycles, and lawn mowers, so I asked him, "Can you fix the dead?"

"Sure-lee."

"Prove it."

"Need something dead first."

My second fish, with the help of some scalding water, died on the spot.

"You gotta pay me," he said.

"How much?"

"Fifteen cents." I paid up. He inspected my money. "Come back tomorrow and it'll be good as new."

The next day, the fish was alive. I suspected it wasn't the same fish, that Figaro had just used my fifteen cents to buy a new one, but I didn't say anything. I just thought how handy he'd be when it came time to resurrect Alice.

When I got home my mother and father were intertwined on the living room couch, kissing. He was the beloved who could take her wherever she wanted to go. It was a kiss full of that belief. I was an incidental lump, unmolded, void of passion. Upstairs, in my room alone, there were no fish, no grandmothers, only the dream of moving my father in the same way.

■

"Figaro," I asked, "when you bring back a dead person are they as sick as before they died?"

"No, they's perfect."

"How much would you charge for that?"

"Oh, that be a pretty penny."

"Over five dollars?"

"No sir. Five dollars oughta jist about cover it."

■

The cigar box only had four sixty-seven.

"Alice, I need some money."

"What for?"

"To pay Figaro."

"Your mother's already paid him."

"Not for yard work, but to bring you back to life. I need thirty-three more cents."

"Well, I don't have it."

"Then gimme some more syringes to sell."

"You have enough syringes."

I looked her in the eye. "Don't you want to come back?"

■

I gave Alice her birthday present though her birthday was still two months away. I'd gotten her a Chinese jump rope. We hooked one end around her feet and the other end around her walker. I jumped in the middle and began the routine. She put her head in her hands and asked, "How's Figaro gonna bring me back to life?"

"I don't exactly know, but look what he did for my fish."

"Will I come back as a fish?"

"Nope. You'll just be you. But there's one condition."

"What's that?"

"You have to tell me everything that happens afterwards."

"Okie-doke." She pulled up her gown and did an imitation of the Charleston.

■

Alice was taken to the hospital on New Year's. I visited her every other day, hair combed and face washed.

"How's the fish?" Alice would ask.

"Fine," I'd say which was only half true.

"I was readin' a magazine the other day," she told me. "It said fish were the first creatures on earth. Tiny microscopic fish that swam out in the desert before there was even an ocean. Then fish grew into dinosaurs then monkeys then people." She looked out at the Arkansas River. "Wouldn't that be something?" The pain on her face was unbearable. "Oh, how I'd swim, child. I'd swim until I just couldn't swim anymore." It was the first time I'd seen her cry.

"What can I do?"

"Don't tell anyone."

■

The next time I saw her she didn't recognize me. Mom shooed me back into the hallway to wait while she tried to get through to her.

Hospital corridors used to have just one sound, the clip of shoes on worn linoleum. Clip, clip, clip. Count the sound from front to finish. Clip, clip, clip.

Alice died that night. I came downstairs the next morning to find my father making pancakes and my mother sitting at the dining room table, all the personality drained from her face. I knew right away. I needed a drink of water so I went to the sink. A pit opened in my stomach as the tap water ran over the glass, down the drain, and past the disposal. Alice.

■

"Figaro, you've got to bring her back." I gave him all my money.

"Got to have a part of her 'fore I can start."

"What kind of part?"

"A fingernail'd do."

■

"I need Alice's fingernail so Figaro can get her back."

My mother was losing patience. "You've got to stop this, Benny. She's dead. There is no coming back."

"But you don't know Figaro. He did it with my fish, didn't he? All I'm asking for's a nail."

A crowd of adults sat around sipping coffee. Uncle Markus and his friend Jack had just gotten in from Ft. Lauderdale. Dr. Granley looked at my mother who told him something with her eyes. He got up and went into the dining room with his doctor bag. The last thing I remember is Uncle Markus refusing to hold me down while Granley gave me a shot.

■

When I woke up the next day, Alice was already buried. The maid was in the room telling Uncle Markus how pitiful it was I didn't have any friends my own age. "Jist spent too much time 'round all that sickness. Don't do you no good."

Uncle Markus asked me if I wanted to go back to Florida with him and Jack for a couple of weeks. We squeezed hands which meant a deal.

The house was full of people. Some laughed, some cried, some ate too much, some got drunk, and they all talked about Alice.

Figaro came up to my room to pay his respects. Under the covers I broke off a nail. "You said you could do it, now do it."

He grinned. From behind his back he pulled out a cut-off milk carton. He poured the contents into my fish bowl: water and a new fish. "This be her. That's all there be to it."

■

It seemed appropriate to feed that fish to the disposal, live, later that night. It seemed appropriate to take the fish bowl out to the backyard and smash it to bits with a hammer. It seemed appropriate to be waiting for Figaro the next morning to demand a refund for what he'd done to my grandmother.

THE I.Q. ZOO

EDELSON, THE TWO-HEADED TURTLE, HAD DIED AT THE
I.Q. Zoo. Randolph was devastated as he shoveled the
dirt over the grave. Edelson had been his friend and
listening ear.

Randolph had never been a pride to anyone. His
mother arranged for him to get a job because he depressed her sitting around the house so much. Why not
give him something to do with his afternoons and week-
ends? Plus ninety cents an hour wasn't bad for a twelve
year old.

"Hurry up out there!" The fat and greasy boss, Joe
Ellis, stood inside the back door.

"Yes, sir." Randolph quickly patted the grave.

"What's taking you so long? Was just a little ol' turtle,
wasn't no pig or dog."

"Be right there, sir."

The round mound OK, Randolph did as he was told.

Ada Su Scull was the only other employee. She ran
the cash register. Lately there hadn't been much need for
her though, hadn't been much business since summer.

She decided to take a break on the I.Q. porch. She ate a bag of Cheetos. Her index finger turned orange. She sucked at it. Randolph came out to talk and Ada Su asked him if he believed in God.

"Doesn't everybody?"

"I don't."

"Why not? He made everything."

"No He didn't. Science did."

Randolph was puzzled. He didn't want to be thinking about that. A lot of the I.Q. animals had died lately, and he liked to picture them in heaven.

The zoo stock was getting low. They were in dire need of a visit from the I.Q. Animal Man. The Animal Man drove from state to state selling superb specimens. Any town could have an I.Q. Zoo if it wanted one: singing dogs, tic-tac-toe chickens, dancing alligators, even freaks like Edelson.

Poor Edelson didn't know any tricks until he met Randolph. He'd been marketed strictly on his heads. The Animal Man said, "A split head's gotta have a split brain and a split brain works too hard against the rest of you. Can't live long like that, but it sure makes you clever in the meantime."

Randolph confided to Ada Su, "I guess it's for the best."

"Death ain't never for the best. That turtle's gonna miss you. You're just gonna have to get yourself a new one."

"Do you think I could teach a new one?"

"Sure you could."

Another turtle made sense. It didn't have to have two heads to be an attraction, not if it could perform the tricks Edelson had. Edelson could turn six somersaults and come out of them saying, "Please." A real "Please," perfectly audible to the human ear.

■

By the time Ada Su got home she was as mad as could be. Some knot tightened around her insides and she couldn't get rid of it no matter what. No matter how much TV she watched, no matter how many records she played, no matter how many times she counted her saved-up money, it was still there.

She went outside for a cigarette and the smoke made her dizzy. She looked up at the moon. Ada Su Scull was a wild dog. She didn't go for that I.Q. Zoo biz.

She stomped down to the cafe where her mama worked. "Gimme a cheeseburger."

Olive Scull had never wanted a child, but supposed if she had to have one it might as well be Ada Su. "Here you go, honey, and with an extra slice of onion."

The kid smiled. So did the mama.

■

The next victims of the Death Plague were the frogs in the Frog Circus. Randolph found them when he went in to feed, Saturday. They were dressed in their little girl out-fits. Death caught them on the Country Club set, their tiny golf clubs abandoned.

Randolph had never cared much for frogs so didn't bother to bury them separately. He just dug a shallow grave and threw them all in.

The work day went quickly. Not much to do with just two chickens and an alligator. He sat on the bench next to the I.Q. gift display. He loved the view from that spot, the busy highway and the colorful billboards.

■

Joe Ellis was out in his warehouse. He had his pants down and was playing with himself. Ada Su sat on a stool ten feet away reading a picture book. Joe Ellis paid her five dollars a session to do just that, plus pretend like she didn't know he was watching. It seemed a good job, a pretty easy way to make five bucks.

She asked him what the matter was. "Why's it taking for goddamn ever?"

"You keep breaking my concentration."

"Well, this is the stupidest book I've ever read." She

flipped through it vigorously. Joe Ellis's pleasure increased. She watched him out of the corner of her eye. His arm was going ninety miles a minute. She couldn't see his privates. She didn't want to either. She could easily go her whole life without seeing them. "My price is going up, Mr. Ellis, starting with today."

"Ssh."

"Ten dollars a time or I'm leaving right now."

His jowls shook. His whole self seemed to vibrate with pressure. She ridded herself of the damn picture book. "Well, it's about time."

■

Randolph heard an agonized squawk. The chickens writhed at the base of the tic-tac-toe machine. "Don't die," he pleaded. "Please don't. You can't die. You just can't."

■

Ada Su got out at the shopping center. "Wait a minute. Mr. Ellis? You keep talking about how you're gonna take me to Little Rock, but you ain't mentioned when. When we gonna go over there?"

"Never knew anybody so excited about Little Rock."

"I wanta see that new airport. They've had it over a year."

"Well, I'm going over tomorrow. Gotta meet with some of my insurance fellas. You can come, but it'll cost you."

"How much?"

"Ten dollars."

"Thief!"

"Take it or leave it."

"What time do we go?"

"Seven." He laughed. "I'll pick you up on the highway."

She gave the door a good slam, then went shoplifting at T.G. & Y. She picked up a brand new version of the fingernail file.

47

In the bowling alley, the banners were up for that night's tournament. Her mama played for Travelers' Insurance. Randolph's mom played for Heights Variety. Travelers' Insurance and Heights Variety were matched in the first game.

■

"Listen Randolph, I may have a party tonight and I may not, but if I do, I do, and I want you to stay in your room." A half-inch ash fell from Vila's cigarette. She flicked it off her nightgown. "Shit."

"Don't worry. I won't bother you none."

"I wish for once you'd disobey me."

He looked at his feet and counted how many times he could shift his weight before she'd say something else.

"If you're hungry, go ahead and fix yourself some food."

Randolph looked for a TV dinner. He'd have that first, then maybe after she left, a chicken pie.

"You're some fat kid."

"You're drunk."

"It's Saturday ain't it? I'm entitled."

"Saturday, Sunday, what's the difference?"

"What do you want from me? You want me to tell you how awful I am? Well I admit it. I'm awful. Now shut up."

Randolph thought about his daddy who'd shot out one of his mom's lungs. Vila shot him back two weeks later when she found him in the garage going at it with another woman. His daddy's picture still sat on top of the TV. Vila squirted it with Windex. Randolph watched the liquid run down his daddy's face.

"What'd you do that for?" he said.

"The glass was smudgy. Get a paper towel and wipe it up for me."

■

Ada Su asked for the hundredth time, "Mama, when are we gonna move some place?"

"Maybe sooner than you think. I aim to buy that dairy

48

bar over in Redfield if my loan comes through."

"You've been waitin' on that for weeks. If you don't hear soon, somebody else is gonna snatch it up before we even have a chance."

"Nothing we can do about that."

"Nothing we can do about too much. It's the only dairy bar in the world built to look just like a pumpkin. And I'm so sick of this place I could die!"

"Be patient, honey."

"I'm not patient! I wanta get to Little Rock. They got ten movie theatres and so many neighborhoods you can't even count 'em all."

"Well Redfield ain't no Little Rock. Besides, there're plenty people who'd give their eyeteeth to live right here."

"I never met any."

"Someday you will, then it'll be too late."

"It's never too late."

"Oh, yes it is."

■

When Randolph was four, he suffered a depression so severe that he stopped responding. He didn't talk. He didn't listen. He didn't sleep, and he didn't seem to wake. They took him to a specialist who confirmed his I.Q. to be normal and his senses fine. His mom told him he was crazy, just as crazy as his crazy daddy.

With Edelson gone, the depression came back. Randolph remembered the visit to the doctor and his mother's lecture. He wasn't going to let anybody know about it this time.

As soon as he fell asleep he dreamt of a new turtle, a turtle the size of a football field. It could squash all of Hot Springs with six somersaults, and when it said "Please," people listened.

■

The bowling ball sped down the lane. Strike. Randolph's mom clasped her hands and swigged another sip of beer. Heights Variety was smearing 'em.

Olive was up next. "That was a nice shot, Vila."

"I really know how to ace 'em, don't I? You might as well drop that ball of yours right into the gutter and save us all the trouble."

"But then again, I might surprise you."

No surprise, though. Olive bowled her usual three.

■

Getting out of the bathtub, Ada Su studied herself in the mirror. She told people she was as ugly a kid as they made, but that was just what she said.

She ran her hands down her sides comparing her reed-like shape to her imaginary friend, Miss Emery. Miss Emery was from Memphis. Miss Emery had long, smooth legs and liked Ada Su to rub them. Miss Emery told her all about the men she knew, but how didn't nothing feel so good as Ada Su rubbing on her legs.

Ada Su, stroking her sides, moved so close to the mirror it fogged over. Her birth certificate, money, and an extra pair of underwear were already packed for the day trip to Little Rock. She wondered if she'd run into Miss Emery at the airport. Better bring along cigarettes, she thought, and leave out the underwear.

■

After the bowl, Vila went over to the Trio Bar. She joined Joe Ellis. "Gonna buy me a drink?" she said, showing off her trophy.

"By the looks of your winnings, you oughta buy me one."

"Hell, this baby ain't worth a dime."

"Bartender? Got a beer for Vila?"

"Pabst, Billy Boy, and make it a cold one."

Vila met her liquid friend head on. "God that's good." Sip. "So, how's my boy working out at the zoo?"

"He does OK."

"I don't want him giving you any trouble."

"I hardly notice him."

"Ain't that the sad truth?"

"He's a good boy."

"Just what I'm afraid of. I'll have him on my hands the rest of my life."

■

Randolph was up at five. He didn't hear his mom or know anything about Joe Ellis being with her. He just got dressed and crawled out the window.

He walked to the part of the highway that went along the Hot Springs Creek. Turtles crossed from one side to the other at dawn. He lay on the side of the road so he could get a good look, eye level.

■

Ada Su was up before Randolph. She was so excited, she made six trips to the bathroom. She ate a Tootsie Roll breakfast and waited for it to be time to go up to the highway.

■

Vila and Joe Ellis had tried to make love but it hadn't gone right. She hadn't slept well. When the sun came up she faked a wheezing fit. Joe Ellis woke in a grog and grunted, "What's goin' on? You OK?"

"Yeah, fine."

Pulling on his trousers, he told her it'd been great.

■

A few turtles crossed the road before Randolph saw the one he wanted. It took its time preparing, didn't crawl out until two pick-ups passed, then set a good pace, strong, scaled legs and hard claws moving steady. It was three-quarters of the way across before it sensed the lurking boy. All movement stopped. Its head withdrew halfway into its shell.

Joe Ellis drove along in a daze. Randolph saw the car and jumped out to grab the turtle. Joe Ellis saw the kid, honked, and slammed on the brakes. The kid heard the honk and jumped back to the side of the road. "What the hell are you doin', Randolph? Tryin' to get yourself killed?" One of the left wheels ran over the turtle. Bits of it splattered on Randolph. He didn't realize what it was at first, and when he did, fainted.

He came to, grabbed the first turtle he saw, and carried it to the zoo.

■

Ada Su paced and fumed, madder and madder. Seven o'clock, no Joe Ellis. Seven-fifteen, he still wasn't there. At eight, she gave up and left. She went down to the I.Q. Zoo and banged furiously on the door.

Randolph heard the banging, but for the longest time couldn't get himself up to answer.

"Where's Joe Ellis?" she demanded to know.

"Little Rock."

"Goddamnit! He was supposed to take me with him!"

Randolph told her about the chickens' death. "All we've got now, Ada Su, is an alligator."

"That's 'cause an alligator don't poison easy."

Randolph looked at her, too dumbfounded to speak.

"You don't think all them animals just died, do you? Joe Ellis poisons 'em. Does it every year. Collects the business insurance to buy new ones. Says if he didn't, people wouldn't come back to see the zoo."

Randolph couldn't believe his ears.

"Hand me a bag of them Cheetos." It was all Randolph could do to pull one off the chip clip.

Ada Su yanked the bag out of his hand. "Damn Joe Ellis. It's one thing to get stood up. It's another thing to get stood up by a creep like him, ruin my whole goddamn day."

She ate the Cheetos, even fed one to Randolph's new turtle. The turtle nibbled at it. "He likes it," she said. Randolph moved farther away. Ada Su dumped out what was left in the bag, then blew it up for popping. She was just about to whack it when she noticed something different printed on the back. It was an entry form. "Goddamn, get a load of this. They're having a Cheeto Contest.

Gimme another bag." Randolph handed her one. "Radios, TVs, they're even giving away a trip to Hawaii." She eyed the chip rack mischievously. "Joe Ellis can fry in hell. I'll get my ownself to goddamn Little Rock. I'll take every pack he's got in this place. I'll win me that trip to Hawaii if it's the last thing I do."

Loaded down, she pranced out proud. Randolph stumbled and landed on the bench. The turtle, sprinkled with Cheeto crumbs, crawled in a circle. Randolph watched it, despairingly. Where would he ever get the strength to teach it anything?

He locked up shop and went home.

The next morning he didn't wake. He lay lifelessly, in a deep, dangerous sleep. Vila thought he was dead, but he wasn't, he was just being Randolph.

Two days went by, three days, four days. His whole heavy being shook, and he wept unconsciously until there were no more tears to be had. He babbled, whimpered, and at times tried to scream out, but the noise just choked in his throat. Finally the fit subsided when exhaustion overrode sorrow. It was as close a thing to hope as he had ever come to.

The deep, silent sleep returned. When he woke, Vila went in to check on him. She didn't know what to think when she saw him jumping up and down on his bed. He'd lost weight. She thought how nice he looked, or was it the booze, she wasn't quite sure. She wasn't quite sure of anything, but Randolph seemed to be. In raising a glass to that boy of hers, she got the shock of her life. Plain as day, he leapt into the air, turned six somersaults, and came out of them saying, "Please."

THE BALLAD OF HANK McCAUL

I OWED JELLY A SONG AND COULDN'T SEEM TO WRITE IT. I just sat there and sat there and sat there. It was all my sorry hotel room's fault, so I slammed out of there to go wander around downtown. I ended up in the pool hall. If an eye-opener with the geezers couldn't get me going, nothing could.

I said a few hellos, then slid onto my bar stool. I ordered a beer and glanced at a copy of the morning paper. The headline said, "Man Sets Self on Fire in Bizarre Claredon Suicide." Claredon was my hometown. I pulled it closer to read the gory details and see if I'd known the victim. Hank McCaul had driven out to the country, pulled off on a side road, and covered himself in gasoline.

I ordered a second beer. I decided to skip lunch and ordered a third, then a fourth, then a fifth, but no matter how much I drank, I still wasn't drunk enough to forget why I'd wanted to be that way. Then someone walked in waving the afternoon edition and said, "Them faggots sure got their asses kicked down in Claredon."

"Let me see that."

The headline was, "Twenty-three Men Charged in Washroom Sex Bust." The names were all listed. Hank's was halfway down.

The last time I'd seen him was at a graduation party twelve years ago. It was the night before I left town. It was also the night he and Phyllis announced their engagement.

Back then I aspired to much more than writing cowboy songs. Like every teenage idiot, I wanted to change the world. I found out living didn't leave much time for that. I was just damn lucky to have Jelly Martin, damn lucky I could put a song down in four-beat heartbreak. Jelly had a publishing company over in Memphis, sold tunes to hillbilly bands mostly. Once in a blue moon he'd even get a hit. A few of them had been mine. Not for a while though.

Jelly had been trying to get me to move to Memphis but I wasn't interested. If I was gonna bottom out, it was gonna be in Little Rock. I don't know what it is about the place, but it's perfect for that. I didn't mind being alone either. It gave me a lot of time to think. I'd just been thinking I had all the answers. The bit with Hank made me think again.

One of the geezers told a joke. The others laughed but the laughter quickly turned to wheezing, hacking, and spitting. I watched my neighbor adjust his suspenders. I listened to him sigh as his heartbeat tried to catch up with the rest of him.

Back in my room, I reread the articles. I kept trying to put some sense to it, but failed and went to bed. Hank showed up in my dreams. It was a rerun of the first time we had sex: the same truck, the same chilly night.

I woke up sweaty and disturbed. I made myself a drink and opened the window. The street was quiet. The air rustled the plastic curtains. I used my bottle to weigh them down.

I'd never given up on the idea that someday Hank would come to his senses. I thought someday I'd be minding my own business and he'd just show up at my door.

■

Because of all the publicity, they buried him the next day. They just had a graveside service. I had a buddy who was pretty good about lending me his car, so I decided to go.

It took over an hour to get from Little Rock to Claredon. I pulled into the cemetery late. Several services were in progress. It took me a minute to find the right one. Phyllis was holding their kids on either side of her. She looked horrible. The only other people there were his parents, some kid I didn't know, and Reverend Weaver of First Baptist.

Mr. McCaul wasn't at all happy to see me. According to him it was my fault Hank ever deviated from God's Great Plan. He had suspected something was going on between Hank and me long before he actually caught us at it, and when he did he sure got his money's worth. He didn't say anything at first. But the next day he told Hank, "If I'm ever convinced I've got a queer for a son I'd just as soon shoot you. And if I ever hear of you so much as talking to Sammy Wills again, god help me, I'll beat the living daylights out of you."

When Hank told me I said, "Bullshit. Surely you're not gonna fall for that."

Too late. He already had.

I went to Madame Ruby's fortune telling trailer and paid her twenty dollars to put a hex on Mr. McCaul. The following weekend he was out practicing target on turtles and shot a hole through his foot. He wasn't supposed to walk on it for at least a month, so he sure as hell wasn't gonna be walking in on me and Hank. But Hank still didn't want to see me.

Hank had a job bagging groceries down at the Piggly Wiggly. I'd wait for him outside the store. He'd walk by like I wasn't even there.

I went back to Madame Ruby's to get her to put on a love hex. She wasn't very sympathetic. I didn't have as much money and she preferred sitting in front of her TV eating pies rather than spending the energy a hex took. I went home and tried to conjure up something on my own.

When I was fourteen I found a copy of a *Life* magazine with a bunch of pictures from the Stonewall Riots. I'd looked at it so much the pages were tattered. It had all these pictures of a bunch of queers, a bunch of rough looking queers fighting the police, the veins on the sides of their necks swollen in the actual pictures themselves from them yelling so hard. I cut those pictures out and mailed them to Hank.

"Let us pray he finds peace in heaven," said the Weave. "Let us pray God forgives his sins. Let us ask Him to forgive us all."

"Amen," I said sarcastically, louder than I'd meant to.

Phyllis glanced at me. Her kids led her to the hearse. I tried to get over to her but Mr. McCaul intercepted me. "We appreciate your comin', Sammy, but we've had about enough to deal with for one day, don't you think?"

"I just wanted to tell her I was sorry. No one else is here to do that."

"I'll tell her for you." He walked over to the car and got in. A moment later they rode away.

Weaver came up and said, "Good to see you, Sammy. You oughtn't stay away from home so long."

"I don't know why, it's never worth the trip when I come."

"That's a pretty lousy attitude."

"It's a pretty lousy place. What do you think it was made 'em go after those guys?"

"They were worried about child abuse."

"That's the oldest excuse in the book."

"There had been a specific complaint. Someone had propositioned a minor."

"How many children were on the surveillance tapes?"

"None, but that's not the point."

"It's not? Hank's dead, Weave."

"You have to be patient with people. The world can't change over night."

"You know damn well what went on in that washroom wasn't anything new. And arresting people isn't gonna stop 'em from having sex. Hell, if there was a way to do that don't you think somebody would have thought of it by now?"

He scratched his palm. "Not all of us are in a position to be as individualistic as you are. I admire it, but it's not something we can all live. Maybe someday, but not now."

"I'll bet it was the new police chief. He used to be in Benton and the same thing happened over there."

"If these men had been at peace with themselves, if they had accepted who they were as many, including you, have managed to do, there wouldn't have been anything to hide, now would there?"

"Like you said, everybody can't live like that."

"What I said was maybe someday—"

"Maybe someday I'll tell everybody about your twelve-inch dick."

He choked. "They'd never believe you."

"But it'd sure give 'em something to think about."

I glanced at the funeral tent. The kid I didn't know was watching them lower the casket. I told Weaver goodbye and went over to introduce myself.

The kid's name was Tom. I asked him if he was old enough to drink. "Wanta go over to the Seventh Wheel?"

"Sure."

"I don't mean to pull you away."

"No, I've had enough of this. Your car or mine?"

"Mine."

■

The Seventh Wheel was famous for its pie and its stench. It was one of those twenty-four hour places that never got cleaned.

We went into the bar section. The jukebox was playing Mel Tillis. I put in my quarter and punched the latest George Strait, then ordered a round.

I asked Tom, "How'd you know Hank?"

"From work."

"Is that all?"

"You mean, am I gay?"

"Not particularly, but is that how you knew him?"

"Well what do you think?"

"I think it'd be a shame if you weren't."

I smiled and he smiled back. I lifted my beer and did my best to sound nonchalant. "How long had you been involved?"

"I wouldn't say we were involved."

"Oh?"

"I might have been, but he wasn't."

"How's that?"

"Hank only took to guys when he was horny, or didn't you know him that well?"

I let that one pass. "Did you have any idea what he was planning to do?"

"No, so don't try to blame me."

"I'm just trying to put it together."

"Good luck."

We avoided each other for a minute. Then he said, "Hank showed me your picture in his yearbook once. He didn't say anything, just pointed it out." Tom looked right at me. Quietly, and with a completely different cadence, he told me, "I teach a swimming class down at the Y. He showed up there a couple of days ago. He'd just come from the police station. They called all twenty-three of 'em in, one at a time, to show 'em the videos. The cameras had been in the heating vents above the cubicles. They asked him what he had to say for himself, told him when his name was gonna be in the paper, then sent him home.

"Hank was pretty calm about it. That should've been the first clue, but I wasn't thinking, I was too busy feeling jealous he was in some t-room when he could have been with me." Tom pulled the beer label off his bottle and pressed it on the bar. "Hank could have fought this thing. The Gay Alliance was down from Little Rock as soon as the story broke with lawyers, everything. But that would have taken too much guts." He'd rolled the label into a ball. He flicked it across the room like a spit wad. It hit the side of the jukebox and stuck.

"It can't be as simple as that," I said.

That remark pissed him off. "It can be however I like."

"Then you're deluding yourself."

"Well, why the fuck not, huh? And what do you know about it? What'd you ever do for him?"

"I loved him."

"Yeah? Did you ever *tell* him that?"

"No."

"Did you ever tell anyone?"

I looked at the different fish that hung mounted behind the bar. Each one was on a plaque with the date, place, and fisherman's name. "'Nother beer?" I said, changing the subject.

Tom looked at me like I'd really let him down. I patted him on the shoulder to prove I hadn't. It didn't work. I tried to smile. Strike three. I excused myself to go pee.

A heavy smell of deodorizer lay over a heavier smell of piss. A lone florescent light rod pulsated on the blink. I looked at myself in the mirror. I ran my hands through my hair then opened my mouth and checked my teeth. I wasn't gonna let any kid get to me, no sir. Nothing was gonna affect me any more than I wanted to let it. I managed to cry before I managed to pee. Then I wondered if anyone was watching me.

When I got back to the bar I told Tom he was right, dead right about me. "I should have told him. I should have shaken him until his teeth rattled. Once when I was in town, I even saw him across the street. He was showing his little girl something in the jewelry store window, but I just walked away, afraid he'd ignore me or wouldn't know who I was. I figured he deserved whatever he got."

I reached for my beer. I picked up my empty instead of my full. Its partner, for a moment, looked like a bowling pin. With the first sip that changed.

Tom said, "Do you ever wonder what it'd be like to settle down with someone?"

"I did when I was younger."

"My age?"

"More like five." We both laughed.

In front of me were two soggy napkins. One stuck to my bottle as I picked it up. I shook it off. The beer foamed over. With my mouth catching it I got a sideways view of the Seventh Wheel's clientele. The whole world may change but the town you come from never will. "You ought to get out of here," I said.

He scooped up my napkin collection, wrung it out in his fist. A gray juice ran down between his fingers. It puddled on the bar. "I plan to. And I'm gonna call you the next time I'm in Little Rock."

■

By the time I got him back to the cemetery we were both good and depressed.

Hank had a visitor. Phyllis was standing by the grave, her hands in her pockets, just staring.

I honked. She waved and walked over.

"Hi, Sammy. Long time no see." She hooked her hair behind her ears. "I sure liked that song you had on the Tanya Tucker album. How ya been?"

"Doin' my best to stay sane."

She laughed halfheartedly. "Well, it ain't easy, is it?" She muttered, "God," then kicked at the ground. "I still can't believe it. I know it's happened but I still can't get used to the idea. The night before last he kept followin' me around the house tellin' me he loved me. The next morning three gallons of gas were gone out of the garage." She looked at my fingers curled around the steering wheel. "Must've been one helluva flame.

"Do you know they left his car outside the salvage shop for a whole day so everybody could drive by and see it? That's the kind of thing that just kills me.

"I know what he was doin' wasn't any more serious than what every teenager in town does parking out on the Bluff, but when I try and explain it—" She stopped. "I gotta get my kids out of here. I'm gonna be movin' over to Tulsa for awhile. I got me a sister over there."

"If there's anything I can do."

"No, I'm just glad y'all came. For Hank and me, both." She leaned against the car, then pushed herself back. One of her belt loops caught on the trim and tore. "Fuck," she said, snapping it off. "If it's not one thing it's something else."

■

Tom and I sat there for the longest time until well after dark. I could only see the outline of his face and the shine of his eyes. I almost said something but just kissed him instead.

"I'll be calling you," he grinned, getting out.

"You do that."

■

I was practically the only one on the road driving back to Little Rock. I told myself it's the lostness of a place that has the final say but I didn't quite believe it.

I stopped off for something to eat before dropping off the car. I walked across Main Street to my shut-down hotel.

I climbed the stairs to my room. I sat on my bed. I poured a whiskey, sipped it, and eyed my suitcase in the corner. I was tempted to pack it and go, and someday I'll do that, someday I sure will. But that night I just sat there until I wrote Jelly his song.

SEX AND LOVE

MEET THIS KID ON THE SUBWAY. SPOT HIM AT WELLESLEY but don't meet him till Bloor. Train breaks down, which never happens on the TTC, but it stalls or something. Car's full. Everybody looks at everybody else. I smile. He smiles back. Scoots down in his seat. Twists his T-shirt in his fingers. Scrapes his beat-up Stan Smiths against the floor. Sexy. And young. Too young. Not my bag, that.

We're almost to an I-see-what-you-see grin when he bunches up his jacket. Puts it between his head and the window. Leans against it and shuts his eyes. Should've been my shoulder. Should've gone right over there.

I look out the window. Can only see the tunnel. I think about the good-old days when you'd meet someone on the subway, have a drink, go home, fuck, maybe get something to eat, then fuck again. I just can't seem to get with it. What with "safe sex" I'm inhibited. Especially with strangers. I mean, there you are in the throes of lust and you've got to stop and have this discussion about condoms, health history, and how deep are you gonna kiss me. So I've just about decided to give up on it. Sex, that is. I've got some good memories. I've even got a lover. Had him over seven years. Our sex life is pretty routine. I keep suggesting we expand our repertoire. Like last week I mentioned investing in a double-headed dildo, something we could do together. But David just makes a face. He says he doesn't need that. I say it isn't a matter of need, maybe it'd be fun. He just shakes his head. David makes a lot of friends on the side. He adores safe sex. Has no problem with it. Even wears a Condoms-Are-Fun button. I say, "Sorry. I'm just not as lucky as you." Then I get a lecture: "It has nothing to do with luck." He tells me to relax more. He says plenty of people are attracted to me, I just don't notice it. "Yeah, people who don't attract me." He says, "Sex comes from emotion. Anyone I like enough I can have fun with." Well maybe, goddamnit, but sex is physical. How can you pretend PHYSICALITY doesn't have all the world to do with sex? David says he loves me. I say I love him too. Then I wonder if it's true. I tell myself, of course it's true. But why do I fantasize so much about leaving? Why do I windowshop for things I'd buy for an apartment of my own? And what about David? Why doesn't any of this ever get to him? He's so happy and well-adjusted it drives me crazy. But it's exactly why I married him. When we met, he was exactly what I was looking for. Exactly.

Train starts moving again. Kid sits up. Looks at me. Smiles this big grin that gets bigger and bigger. I know this look.

I'm fifteen and go over to the scoutmaster's assistant's to get some help on a merit badge. His wife is just leaving to do the Saturday shopping. She's gorgeous. So's he. He gives me a Coke, shows me some Playboys. Then he shows me a magazine with just guys. Rocky and Bullwinkle are on TV. He says he wants to show me something in the attic. He's got this mattress and an old sleeping bag up there. He wrestles me down. Towers over me with his hands on his hips and a great big hard-on in his pants. I'm sort of trembling. He gives me this look so I put my hand on his crotch. Pop that sucker out of his jeans like a jack-in-the-box. We take off our clothes. Make out like crazy. I've always dreamt of this happening and each time I touch him, each time I feel his erection brush against my skin, I have to pinch myself to see if I'm really there. He's massaging my butt. He slips in a finger. It hurts. He whispers, "Relax." He whispers about my prostate gland and asks me if I can feel what he's talking about. I begin to get the idea. He lubricates his penis. It shines like something newborn. He sets my legs up on his shoulders. Enters me slowly. It hurts again for a minute, but as he moves inside of me, he stirs up another sensation altogether. It's like I'm a pinball machine and the jackpot lights up; it's better than anything I've ever felt. He's masturbating me and I come. Five minutes later I come again. He grins. Grunts. Shoots up my insides like magic and hell.

The kid's still smiling like he knows what I'm thinking. I look at him like he's the most precious thing in the world right then.

Go over there, I say to myself. I stand up just as the train pulls into Bloor. I'm suddenly immobilized. Almost get myself pushed out with the exit crowd. The kid looks at me with his eyebrows cocked like question marks. I don't know what to say. He saves me the trouble. "Where you going?" he asks.

"No place really."

"Just riding the subway?"

"That's right."

"What's your name?"

"Kevin. What's yours?"

"Kid." He pats the seat next to him. I swallow. Sit. Stomach's doing a tango. I feel his leg next to mine.

He says, "Wanta come over for lunch?"

"Where?"

"My place."

"You got your own place?"

"My parents, but they're at work."

I'm in the thirty-third floor men's room of the Toronto Dominion Building, locked in a stall, having a good cry about my life. I look at my pants down around my ankles. My white legs. The spots where the hairs have fallen out over the winter. I've just turned thirty. I hate my job. My brilliant career is as far off as it ever was. And I still don't know what to do about David. Lately, we've been talking about a move to the West Coast. Together. But I don't want to be any more together than we already are. Or do I? What I ought to do is move back to New York. David wouldn't follow me there; he hates the States. Christ, any minute I'll be covered in herpes.

Enter Drew Edwards. Flawless, handsome Drew. Twenty-eight, and an associate in the firm where I'm a word processor. I've imagined him seducing me one night when we're working late. I've imagined watching him shower after a good game of racquetball. I've imagined what he thinks about when he masturbates.

I watch him through the crack as he sidles up to the urinal. See him unzip. See his happy face, happy penis, happy pee flowing freely, fingers subconsciously massaging it along, fingers that could have been anybody's, mine even. He finishes, zips himself up, flushes, farts. He washes his hands in the sink, smiles at himself in the mirror. He knows it's me in the cubicle by my pony-fur shoes. He says sarcastically, "Gonna stay in there all day? I've gotta have my Project *K* by two o'clock." He leaves.

I cry some more. For Drew. For how ordinary my dilemma is. For how unspecial I've managed to make myself.

In comes the maintenance man pushing his cleaning cart. He fills the paper towel dispensers. Puts fresh toilet paper in the stall next to mine. Pulls at the door to the one I'm in. Is puzzled to find it locked. He knocks. "Anyone in there?"

I don't answer. He gets down on all fours and looks up at me. "Hey! You deaf or something?"

I still ignore him.

He goes into the next stall, climbs up on the toilet seat, and gestures wildly, "Hey! You!" He throws in a roll of toilet paper. It hits me on the head.

I jump off the john, hitch up my pants, and throw open the latch with the intention of killing that bastard.

I end up in the computer room. My supervisor sees I'm in a state and sits me down in her office. She did a doctoral degree in psychology and asks me a few psychiatric-type questions. Then she deduces, "You couldn't be more normal. Happiness is just a chemical reaction between vitamins, pride, and inventiveness." She smiles. "All you need's a good nutritionist."

Train pulls into Eglinton. "This's us," Kid says. He dodges up the escalator two steps at a time. Past the newsstand. Past the candy kiosk. Hurrying me out to the Flemington Park bus ramp.

The bus is waiting. The driver seems to know Kid. Probably sees him every day. He eyes me suspiciously, so I say, "Fine thank you, and you?" He looks at me like I'm crazy.

At the back of the bus, Kid sinks into his seat with his spine curved into a perfect C. He stretches his legs out in the aisle, his hands to either side of him, one under my thigh. The bus starts moving. He leans over, paves a sidewalk on my neck with his tongue. Mr. Penis fills with blood. Makes me squirm. Kid enjoys this. Sinks even lower into his C to show me his.

I won't tell David about today. He'll say how was work and I'll say fine. I can just see his face. Feel his five o'clock kiss and soft hello suffocate me. Then we'll have a drink like any two reasonable people. Eat dinner. Maybe watch "Dynasty."

"Dynasty" always puts me in a vicious mood. So I'll ask David, in an insinuating tone, if he's seen any of his "friends" lately. He won't say anything. Just his leg will twitch.

All David's friends have one-syllable names. Bob, Rich, Tom, Brad, Jim, Joe. I love it when they call and David's not at home. I know it's one of them by the way they ask for him, hesitating slightly because they know it's me, the lover.

I'm very friendly. "May I take a message?" I ask. Then they give me their one-syllable name. I write it down. "And your number?"

"Oh, he has it." This is where they start to get smug. Little do they realize how many Bobs, Richs, Toms, Brads, Jims, and Joes David knows! I repeat their name with great vigor, before hanging up.

When David gets home, I tell him who's called. He says, "Oh really?" I listen for a trace of guilt, but David never feels guilty. He says, "You know I only see them when I can't see you." I hate that.

Before I go to sleep, I'll manage to blame my depression on the weather. I'll remind myself moving out on my own would be expensive. And who's to say I wouldn't regret it?

Bus turns into an old neighborhood. Big lawns and a mishmash of comfortable old houses. Kid pulls the bus bell. Walks to the door and hops off. People are staring. He says, "Crazy, huh?"

As we walk down the street I see some of his neighbors pacing inside picture windows. They're probably watching some game show. Maybe they're about to win a million dollars. Maybe they're spies and on to me. Maybe they'll call up Kid's mom or dad. Search out my identity. Look me up in the phone book. Come over to my place and put an end to my nonsense once and for all. "How old did you say you were?"

"Aw, don't give me that age trip," Kid says, peeling out in front of me.

I watch his butt. Looks like the butt I caught my first VD from, an airbrush artist I met hitchhiking in San Francisco. I felt like I'd finally arrived as I stood in the VD clinic taking my handful of penicillin. A real homosexual.

The airbrush artist died recently. Of AIDS. I haven't known as many people as some, but I've known enough. I spend a lot of time thinking about it and thinking how glad I am it's not me or David, and what if it is?

I've got a friend who's in the hospital right now. He originally went in because he was losing his vision.

Turned out his eyes were full of Cytomegalovirus. They gave him an experimental antibiotic intravenously, twenty-four hours a day for two weeks. The virus only stabilized. When he got out of the hospital he was thirty pounds underweight. He was back in two weeks later with the same virus plus Kaposi's lesions were beginning to appear in his mouth and on his legs. He got out in another two weeks. He went back again with pneumonia. The latest is that the Cytomegalovirus has moved to his brain.

I visit. We talk about how he feels. How his family's doing. How great all his friends have been. His lover. And thank god for the health care system in Canada. If he'd been in New York, he'd be dead by now.

He lights up a cigarette. "The only thing I haven't managed to quit." He laughs. He's got all these books stacked by his bed on macrobiotics and mysticism. He tells me he's gonna use voodoo to get rid of the Kaposi's. He says, "To think of all those hours I spent in school on things like math and chemistry when I could've been learning how to grow my leg back—"

I find I'm crying. He says, "Hey, I'm OK. Listen, I don't want you worrying about me." But he doesn't understand. It's not so much his illness. It's his guts. It's that I love him and I'm afraid to say it. Afraid he will think it false.

The AIDS Committee is holding a twilight vigil in Cawthra Park. I don't really want to go, but at the same time, I don't want to miss it. They seem to have a talent for picking the whiniest, most uninspirational speakers, and god could we use some inspiration. The Committee's president looks like he hasn't had a bath in weeks. To lend effect to his funding plea, I suppose. The sister of a guy who died recently reads a prayer. Divine Will and love. She stumbles over the words. A local chiropractor, in the pink of health, sings an original folk song in a very original key. He tries to get everyone to sing along, but no one does. A rock 'n roller in a high-rise hollers down, "Faggots!" The crowd acts deaf. Only a few heads turn to see who's said it. If I were an AIDS ghost I would've pissed on them all.

Finally we are instructed to light the candles we've bought for a dollar's donation. As the crowd disperses, people stick them into the ground. The wind blows them out instantaneously.

I spot David. He's come from a meeting and is standing with some of his political cronies. He seems as depressed as I am.

I try to imagine a vigil worthy of the people I've known. I see something at Radio City Music Hall. Thousands of AIDS patients. In a chorus line. Sick and skinny and can-canning across that great stage. They're outfitted like the Rockettes and have long, flowing wigs. They stop to face the audience and sing a choral version of the aria Tosca sang to God: "I lived for art, I lived for love/never did I harm a living creature . . ./Ever in pure faith my prayers rose/Ever in pure faith . . ./Why dost thou repay me thus?" It raises the roof, literally. Out they fly, one by one. A million Peter Pans, free at last.

Kid unlocks his door. "Don't steal anything, OK?" A portrait of a much younger him hangs in the hallway.

"Haven't changed much, have you?"

"It's my mom." He takes my coat. "Let's go upstairs."

The walls are lined with pictures from his birthdays, piano recitals, various school trips. His room's a mess, clothes piled in the only chair. There's an autographed poster of Domaso Garcia tacked to the wall.

"Baseball fan?"

He shrugs. "I just think he's cute."

He plops down on his bed, kicks off his Stan Smiths. Hooks his thumbs in my belt loops. Presses against my crotch. Blows through the material, hot enough to feel. Mr. Penis is in bondage. I reach in to make an adjustment. Kid leans back on his elbows and presses Mr. Penis with his foot. Size 8.

I pull off his socks. White cotton scented slightly with his sneakers. I lick his toes. He giggles and grabs for me, but I dodge him. I lick the arch of his foot. The sole. The heel. His skin is so soft. My hands glide beneath the cuffs of his jeans to see if all of it feels the same or if the quality changes with the hair on his legs, but no. I lick his fingers. Wish he were an octopus. Wish for more appendages to devour. More of him to wrap around me as I descend. Hand in his shirt. The smoothness of his back. Hand slipping down. Slipping to the waistband of his jeans. Unbuckling them. Slowly. Peeling off his underwear. Pale pink Calvin Klein's. His cock, so full. So sweet to kiss and sweet to swallow. He'll be catalogued with all the great genitals I've known. To be called upon when I'm alone and need them most.

"Stop," Kid whispers, tongue in my ear, freezing. "Too close." Wants a kiss is all.

He dives under the covers. Works his way up my length. To my crotch. Lifts my legs. Outlines my ass. Spits on his fingers. Gives me one. Gives me two. Sees my eyes roll. Gives me three.

He kisses me like crazy. I pull him on top of me. Slap his butt. Tug his nipples. Eat the vein along his neck. His penis, against my thigh, springs between my legs.

David and I are in a restaurant having dinner. I wanted to go to a different one but he insisted we try this. The lights are too bright, fluorescent. The food is too dull and costs too much. Too many people are smoking. I hate the way David's looking at me. As if I'm supposed to supply some feeling or dialogue to make the evening a good one. I hate the way he eats.

We walk down the street together. Get on the subway together. Get cruised together. Get off together. Go across the parking lot to our building together. Ride up the elevator together. Walk into our apartment together. Listen to the messages on our answering machine together. Kill cockroaches together. Brush our teeth together. Get in bed together.

I pick a fight for no good reason just before he falls asleep, then get furious with him for letting me do it.

I lie there trying to remember a movie or a play where two characters are stuck in the how-it'll-probably-be-again-but-isn't-now sort of thing. But all I can remember is new romance. Adventure, fire, sex, meetings on the sly.

Or breakups, the more violent the better. Or Gina Rowlands going off to the loony bin. Or kids on the subway. Or scoutmasters' assistants. But never what really happens between people. I mean, who cares about that?

Best not to know anyone too well. When you do you just have the same boring problems you always have.

Kid rips open a condom pack with his teeth. Kneels in front of me. Pulls it on without the least bit of fumbling. Grins from the tickle of the lube.

"You're quite adept at that."

"Learned it from a friend of my uncle's," he confides.

Love the whites of his eyes. His kiss getting vicious. His hands digging into my shoulders. The spit on his teeth. The smile that breaks on his breath. The cum that fills the rubber that should be filling me.

I look deeply into his eyes. He lets me. We fall in love for about five minutes.

He says, "Nice."

"Yeah."

He rolls over. Sighs. Feels like he has to say, "This friend of my uncle's"—he pushes his hair out of his eyes— "we're kind of involved."

"Listen, don't worry. I've already got a lover."

David and I are kissing passionately in our sleep. When we wake up, we stop. Our breath is sour. We look at each other like strangers. The room is full of a shadowy half-light. "I love you," I finally say, "don't you know that?"

"Let me make you a sandwich," Kid says, slipping on a pair of gym shorts. He goes into the bathroom and comes back with his father's robe. He hands it to me.

In the breakfast nook he tells me he has to write a paper for his physics class. That he was supposed to work on it this afternoon and'll probably be up all night. Then he says, "I'd like to get together again sometime, if you would."

"Sure, whenever. You could even come by my place."

"What about your lover?"

"He's out of town a lot."

"Live anywhere near Jarvis Collegiate?"

"Two blocks." I grin.

He leans back in his chair, holding onto the edge of the table for balance. "The nature of infinity," he says, rocking.

"I beg your pardon?"

"The paper I've got to write. The universe going on forever. From way off in outer space right down to the tiniest dot on your fingernail."

"Sounds complicated."

"It's not."

The sandwich is finished. Our plates are in the sink. Kid undoes his father's robe. Slips it off my shoulders. Stands in front of me just short of touching, yet I can feel his temperature, the tips of his toes, and his penis again getting hard.

We go into the bathroom. Get in the shower. Keep soaping up until the smell of cum makes us dizzier than even the steam.

"My parents'll be home soon," he says as we dry.

We stand in the entrance hall. He's written his phone number on a slip of paper. He folds it in half and tucks it in my pocket. "Call. OK?"

I'm back on the subway. David and I are coming home from a dinner party. We're slightly drunk and having a jolly old time talking about who was there.

We get into our apartment. I put on some show music. The overture swells and we begin to dance, dancing a little dance that only we know the steps to.

WILMA'S WEEK

YOU GET TO WORK MONDAY MORNING. YOU'RE LATE. There's a message on your desk from your doctor. You've been waiting for this call your whole life, dreamt of it, imagined it. You pick up the phone to call him back. Your boss wants you to take dictation right away. You put the phone down. You'll try again on your break.

Your break comes. You get a cup of coffee, then dial the number. "It's Wilma Rhine," you announce to the receptionist. Your name has a false ring.

"Oh yes," she says. "Doctor would like to see you. As soon as possible."

"Is something wrong?"

"I wouldn't know. I just make the appointments. How's four o'clock?"

"Fine."

Of course there's something wrong. Doctors don't just call you in for no reason. You think of all those tests you had done: blood, urine, feces—this cell, that cell. You giggle. You inform your supervisor you'll be leaving early. "Doctor's appointment."

The doctor sits you down, asks if you're comfortable. You say, "So-so."

He clears his throat and announces the news: "You're dying."

You smile, thank him, then go home.

You look at yourself in the mirror. You pull at your face. What exists? What doesn't? You turn on the faucet, splash cold water on your skin. You flush the toilet even though it doesn't need it. You call your mother, but she's in Mexico. You eat, bathe, watch TV. You try to read but cannot concentrate; you can only think of one thing: death.

You dream about your grandmother who lived and lived until no one knew her. Every couple of years, guilt drew you to her bedside. She lay in a nursing home, in a grandmother-sized crib. As a gift you'd take her a candy bar. She'd unwrap it full of delight and pleasure. She'd put it under her nightgown and press it against her belly where it would melt, then reharden over her skin. When she felt like a bite she'd just peel some off.

Tuesday morning there's no message waiting for you so you figure your doctor's news still stands. You're too distracted to work, but type away all the same. There are reports to be drafted and filing to be filed and graphs to be filled in and appointments to be made. Your boss is in one of his moods. You still cannot abide them even though you've done so for six years. Even though you've been through his divorce, his Christmases, his birthdays, alcoholism, girlfriends, golf lessons, tennis lessons, squash lessons— you still can't stand it. Today is the day you write out his kids' checks. You write them and he signs. When the brats call to complain that it's not enough, you calm them down. Your job suits you even less than your name. You knock on your boss's door.

"What is it?" he bellows.

"I want a raise."

"How much?"

"As much as I can get."

"I've already OK-ed you for four percent."

"I want at least eight."

"Gimme one good reason why."

"Gimme one good reason why not!"

You stare it out. Finally you add, "I'm pregnant."

He smiles. It's far from a smiling smile, more of a program simply forced upon the face. "Congratulations," he says. "We'll go to lunch."

"What about my eight percent?"

"I'll see what I can do."

You walk out.

"Hey!" he says. "When's your leave?"

"I'll speak to personnel."

"So will I."

At five, you go home. You get a glass of sherry and mix in a teaspoon of poison. It's concocted for you personally by a psychic in Mill Valley and is by far the most interesting approach to death. Totally painless, the symptoms imitate disease. It won't affect your life insurance one bit. Gingerly, you tap the spoon against the glass.

You take a comfortable chair in the living room. A huge chunk of ice hits your roof, crashes through, and lands not three feet from where you're sitting. You, totally amazed, get drunk.

Later, you call a girl from work and tell her about it. She tells you you're dreaming. You decide she's right and go to bed.

The ice is still there in the morning. You call the fire department. They come and confirm it to be ice indeed and speculate it fell from an airplane somehow.

It's not long before the newspapers get wind of the story. They come for an interview and to take some pictures. You don't get to work until midafternoon.

Most people hate Monday or Tuesday, but for you, it's Wednesday. It's the limbo, the two days down and two days to go. It's usually on Wednesday that you recall your old ambitions: your writing career and your acting career. You ride the bus gazing out the window at the fog. You wonder where you might have gone, could have gone had your luck been different.

On your way into your building you pick up the afternoon paper. You and the ice chunk are on the front page. You, of all people.

The telephone rings off the hook. Everyone in town calls to tell you they've seen it. Then they ask, "So, by the way, how are you?"

"I'm just fine," you say. You're not telling anyone about your death.

Your brother calls. He's why you moved to San Francisco in the first place, but you've never told him that and he's never guessed. You live two neighborhoods apart but only see each other sporadically, when there's a family crisis, lonesome holiday, or something totally out of the ordinary like the ice cube.

"Wilma! Saw you on the front page of the *Examiner.* Way to go!"

"Wasn't that something?"

"What are they gonna do with it?"

"Let it melt, I guess."

"They ought to put it in the science museum. It could be from outer space."

"No, Shawn. They did ice last year. This year it's dinosaurs."

"Well, if it were me, I'd chip off chunks and sell 'em down at the Wharf."

"Well I'm not you, thank god."

He laughs. "I take it you're still not ready to join me in the real estate business?"

"No way."

He invites you to come over for a drink the following afternoon. "Did you get a postcard from Mom?" he adds.

"Not yet."

"Remind me to show you mine."

Just as you hang up your boss comes out of his office. "No raise. I talked to personnel. You're not pregnant. I've got no time for bullshit."

You stare into space. On your screen the letters jumble and fall like paratroopers. You give the command to display page after page. You look at all that work, letter after letter, then stumble on your lone short story, your still unfinished masterpiece. "Confession" it's called. What a bunch of crap.

When you get home you discover your neighbors have let their Dobermans out on the roof again. There they are, growling at you through your skylight, pawing at the glass, trampling on it. Thank god the landlord's fixed the ice hole or they'd have gotten inside. You growl back. That makes them even madder. Any minute they'll come crashing through and eat you alive. There ought to be a law against people keeping dogs like that.

Once you almost killed a Doberman. You were at Shawn's with a dog of your own. You took your mutt out on the fire escape to look at the view. A Doberman, bounding up the stairs, jumped your dog. His owner, a hippie lady, said nothing. You thought her dog would kill your dog, so you tried to kick them apart. Your kick threw the Doberman off balance. He slipped off the landing, dangled for an instant by his front paws, then fell three floors down into the yard. The hippie lady screamed bloody murder at you. Please let the dog live, you prayed. You looked over the rail. The dog, only slightly stunned, was standing up. Soon, he was running back up the stairs to reattack your dog.

Shawn had just moved there after moving out on Mike. You missed Mike. "How can you throw away six years?" you said.

Shawn said it was because he was too fickle to let himself be loved. He said his psychiatrist told him it all stemmed from how the two of you had been brought up. He had analyzed it from every angle, he assured you, and maybe that was the problem. He said what you have to do is ask yourself what it is you love about your lover aside from his loving you. He asked if you followed this. You said "yes" but weren't entirely sure. You said "yes" again for emphasis.

"I just want somebody new, somebody sexier, somebody who doesn't know me so well."

"What if you're throwing away your one big chance?"

"What if you're really dying like you're always saying? There're thousands of people, Wilma, thousands. Quit worrying about me and find someone for yourself."

"I don't want anyone. Besides, there aren't any straight men in San Francisco."

"There are on Union Street."

"I hate Union Street."

"Then get a woman."

"Thanks, but I need my time to write."

The Dobermans are still growling when you crawl into bed.

Thursday isn't as bad as Wednesday. That's what gets you up. There's nothing left of the ice chunk except what you saved in the freezer. You pack it with your lunch. You'll put it in the fridge in the employee's lounge and take it as a present to Shawn.

You're late, ten minutes. Your boss is already buzzing you when you get to your desk. His mail needs opening. Is there anything from Cybernetics? You look. No. You sit down to transcribe one of his incoherent tapes. He buzzes you again. You get up. "What is it?" you snap. You haven't had enough coffee to disguise your irritability.

"I think you need a transfer back to the typing pool. Your attitude is inexcusable."

"I'll try and do better."

"It's too late for that."

"Is it because of my baby?"

"Are you having one or not?"

"That's none of your business. All that should concern you is whether I do my job."

"In my view, you don't."

"I'm more efficient than anyone else on this floor."

"Nobody's indispensible. I had six reports go up to Tommy with typos. You didn't proof them."

"That's your job."

"Your job, Wilma, is to catch what I miss. And another thing, my wife saw that story about you in the paper. Was it really necessary to mention the firm? I shouldn't have to tell you gigantic ice chunks are incongruent with a stable financial image."

"They just asked me where I worked."

"It's a matter of maturity. Perhaps you could benefit from professional help."

You go back to your desk. You get out all of his disks. You spend the morning blanking them out, one by one.

You hide in the supply room. You stack and restack packages of Xerox paper, waiting it out till five.

The minute you get to Shawn's he gives you a strong margarita and a bowl of guacamole. You had forgotten how pleasant life could be. You appreciate the reminder.

"I've got tickets for the theatre tomorrow night," he says. "They're doing *Hay Fever*. Wanta go?"

"I thought you had tickets with Phil."

"He's in Seattle."

"Then sure."

"Dinner at Café Americain?"

"You just love dragging me to restaurants I can't afford."

"You've gotta eat somewhere."

You change the subject. You tell him you've almost finished a new story.

"What's it about?"

"A woman who's dying, who's always wanted to die, and is finally getting to."

"Oh, Wil-ma."

"Don't call me Wil-ma, Shawn. God! I knew I shouldn't have told you."

"No, I'd like to read it. Really." He tops off your margarita.

You think of all the things you've given him to read in the past: books, papers, articles. Not once can you remember him ever mentioning actually having read one. Maybe he doesn't read at all. Maybe he never learned how. He's put entirely too much margarita in your glass. You catch it with your finger, suck it off. "Don't get me drunk," you say. "I've got work to do."

He keeps pouring. "You work too hard."

"You work much harder than I do."

"But I don't take it as seriously. And I make twice as much money."

"Shawn, I enjoy my unhappiness. If it makes me happy why should you mind?"

You walk home. You arrive feeling more agitated than before you set out. You drink some hot milk, watch the news. You watch the opening of *The Tonight Show*, but turn it off at the first commercials. You try to sleep. Again and again you're almost there, but your adrenalin won't let you. At three a.m. you turn on the light, walk over to your closet. The top shelf is full of suicide tricks: pills, ropes, plastic bags, wires, even a gun. You haul them down and spread them on your bed. You fondle them, distribute them beneath the covers. You'll have to get rid of them soon, but for now you make your bed with them inside it, then lie on top.

In the morning you sleep through your alarm. You don't become aware of it until nine-thirty. It's part of your dream, the incessant buzzing, then you realize, this is no dream.

You ought to call work and let them know you're on your way but you don't.

You're in the elevator going up. The idiot file clerk gets in. She chatters and chatters. You look at her, your lip curling in disgust that any human being could be so tedious, so insensitive, so utterly stupid.

You walk onto your floor and see your boss in a panic standing over some temp who's inserting his disks into your machine. "Nothing to display," says the prompt.

He's livid. "Where is it? Where the hell is it?"

"Obviously it's been lost," you say. "I've told you not to put a temp in my place."

"Lost? What do you mean, lost?"

You explain how the temp must have done something to cause the machine to ruin the disks. The temp is in tears. She has no comprehension how she might have done such a thing but takes full responsibility. Your boss yells and yells, "What about the Project Report? What about my Wild Bill Contract? Jesus fucking Christ. Idiots!"

Some small angelic particle in you takes pity on the poor temp. You look at your boss. "I erased your goddamn disks yesterday. If I go to the typing pool, I'll take you with me."

His face turns redder and redder. He tries to fight it but lifts an arm to strike. He'll knock the insolence out of you, and if that doesn't work, he'll hit you again and again until it does. You're proud to provoke such a response. His backhand comes so close to your face he can feel your smile. The secretaries gasp. He catches himself. He storms into his office and slams the door. Everyone's still staring. You shout, "So what the hell's the matter?" Quickly, they go back to whatever they were doing.

On your telephone, your boss's line lights up. You listen at his door. He's talking to personnel. No typing pool. You dismiss the temp, full pay. You call the deli downstairs and order everyone a muffin, bran. You pass them out, one per desk. No one touches them. By Monday they'll be paperweights.

The day drags on. You haven't felt so egged on by dullness since grade school. You stare at the clock. Your mind is a million miles away but you must sit there until thirty minutes, then twenty minutes, then ten minutes have passed.

You start asking people what they think the meaning of life is. They look at you like you're crazy. They haven't time for this, but you insist, "No, really, what's the first thing that comes to your mind when I say, 'What is the meaning of life?'"

Your boss and the other partners wave you off with their usual irritation, but you're undaunted. The associates, for the most part, answer. Most of them say, "I don't know." A few say "success" or "money."

You ask the secretaries and the file clerks. They think about this a lot. Their answers are much more colorful: "a can of Pepsi," "a couple of pretzels," "a TV show," "love," "birth," only a few say, "I don't know."

By the photocopy machine, the girl you called about the ice chunk says, "So what do you think it is, asshole?"

"What?" you ask.

"The meaning of life."

"There isn't one," you say happily.

The girl is putting on lipstick using the shiny part of the binder machine as a mirror. "What else is new?" She blots, then offers it to you.

"Never touch the stuff."

"That's your funeral, not mine, but you could use a little help."

You take it. Draw on huge lips with wild abandon. Disgusted, your "friend" grabs it back and leaves. You go to the ladies' to scrub it off. When you come out, everyone's gone.

You sit down to work on your story. You read through the opening paragraphs and decide they're shit. You hit the cut key. You read on. The heroine's no longer pregnant. You cut that paragraph too. She doesn't drink, doesn't smoke, doesn't fuck, doesn't fall in love. She has no vices of any sort. Her purity is luminous, you write, and that is why she must die.

You stand up and walk to the window. You look at the street full of traffic, a sea of tail lights stalled on Friday night. You look at the skyscape, the Berkeley Hills across the bay. You look at the office, the clutter: files, papers, muffins that wink at you from desk to desk. You pass the cleaning women on your way out. You say, "Hello." She ignores you.

When you get to the theatre your foot starts hurting. You hope it's not that damn hangnail on your baby toe. At intermission Shawn tells you you're pale. "And what's that faint red mark all around your mouth?" You wouldn't mind explaining, but he wouldn't understand. Plus your toe's still hurting.

Afterwards, you end up at Café Americain anyway. Shawn says he'll pay. He thinks you should drink more. You listen to him tell you all about it, then let him order. He's talking non-stop. He always does this when he thinks you're down, but you're not particularly down. He's never understood you and never will.

Dinner is delicious. You even manage half a dozen laughs before he drops you off. You thank him genuinely. "Night," you say.

You get into your apartment and immediately kick off your shoes. You pull off your damn panty hose and inspect that nagging toe. The nail's split again, part of it digging into the flesh. You pick at it. It starts to bleed. You mop it with a Kleenex. Your baby toenails are slowly disappearing. A millimetre at a time, they peel off and don't grow back. It's a living testimony of evolution, you decide. Damn thing. You pick at it and pick at it and pick at it.

SUCCESS

Goo Riley stood in the sad beauty of a West Virginia downpour. His thumb was out toward Charleston but nobody would stop. Finally he decided, fuck it, and walked up the on-ramp to a service station cafe. He took a seat at the counter.

The waitress was friendly. "Pretty wet, huh?"

"A killer."

"Rained out the parade we was s'posed to have. The tenth anniversary of the end of Vietnam. Even had us a float. Had six vets to ride on it and two of 'em were amputees."

"Shit."

"What do you mean, shit?"

"Just shit, that's all."

"You weren't in the war, were you?"

"What if I was? Ain't no different from nothin' else. No better, no worse. Everybody oughta know how to 'preciate a good nightmare, right?"

"Right. So whatcha gonna have?"

"Coffee."

"Wanta look at the newspaper?"

"No thanks."

She set one in front of him anyway. He covered it with cream.

"Now what'd ya go and do that for?"

"'Cause I don't care."

"What if someone else wants to read it?"

"Tell 'em to see me."

She busied herself with her side work and left him alone until his third refill. Then she said, "I lost my fiancé in Vietnam. I get off in another few minutes. Wanta buy me a beer?"

"Can't afford it."

"Then let me buy you one."

"Couldn't do that."

"You couldn't?" She sashayed into the kitchen. Goo heard her tell the dishwasher, "Say, Wade, I done found me an honest-to-god gentleman. Don't look like much of one, but he didn't even grin when I mentioned my money." She returned to the counter smiling. "Tell ya what, honey, you have yourself another cup of coffee and gimme a minute to change."

Goo watched the rain beat against the window. His face had the expression it usually had when he was on the verge of some luck. Luck didn't like Goo.

His head hurt. He hadn't eaten. Coffee and cigarettes just didn't do it somehow. If he could just get the waitress to give him an egg, a raw one to mix in the bottom of his cup, he'd be fine. He thought to call her over, but was reminded of his wife.

Everybody thought keeping his promise to marry Betty had been the last good thing he could credit himself with, but Goo wasn't at all convinced. When he came home from the war, he knew it wasn't right. He only went through with it because of all the plans she'd made. That, he figured, was love, or a start anyway.

To Betty, Nam was a mild irritant, better off ignored, one of the sad things that happened in a world that could be perfect if you didn't think about it much. Goo hated her innocence. He hated the glaze it put on her eyes, a glaze that belonged on cakes and candies, not women or men. He took it out on her with sex. She bled bad their first night and cried, but Goo didn't care. He stayed on her like a dog. He slept late the next morning. When he woke, she was gone. He had to admire her for that. At least she had the guts to get up and go. Then in she walked, loaded down with souvenirs from the motel's gift shop, presents for her parents and brothers and sisters. "We're gonna have a good life, aren't we Goo? Tell me we are."

A year later, he left.

By then they'd concocted a baby, a retarded, malformed lump. All the secrets in the world were locked in that kid. Goo could see it in his eyes and hear it in the sounds he made when he was hungry or wet. The baby was the only thing he told goodbye. He stood over the crib and burned with jealousy. How he envied his impenetrable shell.

The waitress returned in time to see Goo vomit.

"Honey, are you all right?"

He retched once more then wiped off his mouth. "Fine."

She pulled a rag out of the bus tray and threw it over the mess. "Don't look like you've had solid food in a week. Need me to get you something?"

"An egg."

"Just an egg?"

"If you've got any."

"Sure, we got eggs. Lots of 'em."

He ate it raw just like he'd imagined. It tasted perfect and he thanked the waitress.

She took him up to the room she lived in above the cafe. The shades that covered the windows were thin and old. Every time a car went by headlights bled across the walls like a movie.

They undressed. Goo kept on his shorts; she kept on a T-shirt. She made the first move. From behind, she put her arms around him. She whispered, "Tell Donna Jean what you're runnin' from."

"Ain't runnin' from nothin'."

"Just runnin' to run then?"

"If that's what you want to call it."

"We're lookin' for a breakfast cook. Interested?"

"No."

"Will ya think about it at least?" She kissed the back of his neck, then reached in the front of his shorts. "Ya got a nice body, know that? I bet you could be one looker if somebody'd give ya a bath and a shave." She found his nipples and caressed them. She caressed the tired muscles of his chest and stomach. One hand went to his face, the other to his balls. "I'm just a friendly sorta girl. Get's dull in this burg. Horny, anything wrong with that?" She pushed him down on the bed, pulled down his shorts, and climbed on. "We fit good," she said, setting the rhythm. He lost his erection. She managed to come anyway, then got up, and wiped. She looked prettier than before. She took hold of his soft penis. "You're not queer, are you?" She took him in her mouth. "Let's bet on it. Got a quarter?"

"How come you wear that T-shirt?" Goo asked her.

"To cover my scar."

"What kind of scar you got?"

She showed him. The skin from her left breast to her right abdomen was a molten swirl.

"Hope you sued."

"Sue who? It was my own damn fault. I's only tryin' to kill myself."

Goo lay his head on the pillow. "Why?"

"No exact reason. Just tired of it all."

Goo smiled. He fell asleep. When he woke up twenty minutes later, she was going through his pockets. "What the hell are you doing?"

"Just lookin' to see who you are. You ain't even got any ID." She sat on the bed. "You had a hell of a dream. I thought you was gonna hit me. I don't go in for that." She stretched out. "Let's discuss my offer?"

"What offer?"

"The breakfast cook."

He got up.

"Where you goin'? You can't go anywhere. We're perfect for each other, can't you see that? We ought to do something crazy. Like get married. What do you say?"

"I already am married."

"Well, nobody 'round here'd know that. All you'd have to do is stand there and say yes." Goo laughed at her. She laughed back, then went over to the window, opened it, and hollered out, "Hey everybody, me and the new breakfast cook's gettin' hitched!" She turned toward him. "Sounds pretty good, don't it? What's your name, anyway?"

Goo didn't answer.

When the door shut behind him, she hit it with a chair.

■

Kate Cruickshank dug her pistol out of her sweater drawer. Her daddy had given it to her when she turned sixteen. She'd only used it a couple of times: once on a raccoon who wandered into the back yard, and once on her little sister's cat. She wondered if she still had any aim.

She put it between some magazines and walked out of the bedroom. She passed her husband watching his ball game and turned down the hall.

"Whatcha doin' baby?"

"Just goin' out to the garage to work on my chair." Kate refinished furniture.

"It's too cold."

"Don't worry. I got me a sweater on."

She locked the door. She covered her work bench with newspaper, laid down the gun, and got out some oil. She went over to the rag bin and pulled out a piece of her old granny gown. Somebody'd given it to her as a joke for marrying a man old enough to be her father. Kate met Codder at Emily Cruickshank's eighteenth birthday. Codder rented a party barge, took ten of 'em out on the lake. A year later, they eloped to Las Vegas. They announced their marriage at the breakfast following her debut. The heartbreak on her parents' faces had been worth it all.

She adored the granny gown. She wore it mostly on Saturday mornings as she watched her cartoons. She was addicted to them. Codder kidded her about it. But wasn't that what he wanted? A nymphette, a little girl to dress up, then molest?

The day she turned thirty his interest began to wane. Not that she cared. She was relieved at first, but jealous when it dawned on her he had someone else. It didn't matter that she had someone too. It was the principle of the thing: who humiliated whom first.

Everybody in town had heard the rumors about Codder having his first wife knocked off. Kate had heard him say a thousand times, "Murder's a lot cheaper than divorce." He always said it as a joke, but her better senses took warning. Kate was pretty sure he knew about Angus. She was also pretty sure he was having her followed. He'd been acting much too confident lately.

She slipped on a pair of calf-skin gloves and aimed the pistol at the garage door. "Click," she said, watching the imaginary bullet.

She buried the gun in the rag bin. She put the rags she used to clean it with in the trash, then picked up the newspaper. She looked at the front page article on the tenth anniversary of the end of Vietnam. Washington had a new monument. God, was it ugly. Just a bunch of names on a long black stone.

■

The first time Goo attempted to shoot himself, he shot his reflection in the mirror. Betty ran in to see what had happened. Goo pointed the gun at her thinking of the carnival man, the knife thrower who throws knives at his lovely wife. He repeated the phenomenal trick by shooting the remaining bullets: two to Betty's left, two to Betty's right, and one just above her head.

Betty stepped from the target in a daze, then she became hysterical. "You could've killed me," she screamed, "You could've killed me dead!" She threatened to call the police, but when it came down to it, never did.

A pickup pulled over. The driver honked and hollered, "Say buddy, you hitchin' a ride or what?" Goo trotted toward him. "Run, you mother fucker, run!"

"Where you goin'?" Goo asked.

"New Albany."

Goo got in.

The driver was a hunched-over man with a crewcut and a squint. Goo took a cigarette butt out of the ashtray and lit it. He watched the rain on the windshield and wondered what it'd be like to own this truck, or better yet steal it. He figured he'd have to kill the guy to get it, stab him six, maybe seven times, then dump him in some ditch. He'd listen to the radio to see when they said something about a body being found, or maybe he'd just keep it with him. How much could this old fart stink anyway? "Shit," Goo chuckled.

"What?" the old man said.

"Just thinkin'."

" 'Bout what?"

" 'Bout killin' you."

"Hell." The old man laughed. "You wanta git out and walk?"

"No sir."

"Then shut up and take the ride in peace."

■

Codder wanted to barbecue. Kate told him it was too wet. Codder said that didn't matter and went out to start a fire. He set up the coals, then went to the garage to get his electric starter. He looked at the trash can overstuffed with newspaper and oily granny gown rags. He fingered the rags. He made a mental note to ask Kate not to use such good ones refinishing.

Kate berated him for being so insistent about a barbecue when they had plenty of other food to eat. She could heat something up. Didn't he want her to make something nice? No, he wanted a barbecued steak. She called him a damn brat. She was prepared to make an issue of it, but remembered it was his last meal, so she let it drop. She felt a pain in her abdomen and excused herself. She suffered diarrhea. Nerves.

Mac Searcy dropped by. He and Codder were in the process of stopping some local real estate investments by a group from Cincinnati. Kate thought he'd never leave. The drunker they got the more Mac watched her. "Sure got a pretty looking wife," he said.

"Hell, you can have her." Codder laughed. His jowls shook like an old bulldog.

Kate went to the bedroom and picked up the phone. She called Angus down at his Texaco station. "Better not come up for another couple of hours, baby. We haven't even eaten yet."

"Say 'bout midnight?"

"That oughta be fine. But meet me up at the barn. And don't bring your car. I can't wait to see ya. I'm just about to jump outta my skin."

Codder went out to check his grill. The coals still hadn't caught. He yanked the electric starter out and waved it in the air. "Damn gizmo's supposed to work no matter what!" He threw it in the shrubs.

Kate watched through the kitchen window. She slapped on a skillet. "Now, gimme that steak."

He ate. She didn't. She just drank. After her third bourbon she felt drunk enough to relax. She plopped down in the den with a fashion magazine. Kate was the only person in Lavalette who even remotely resembled a model. She smirked. She watched Codder take off his shoes and socks and put his chair in the recline position.

Codder Cruickshank had the ugliest feet his wife had ever seen.

■

"Hell, people are just great," the old man said to Goo, "that is if you know 'em right. I help you; you help me. That's the way it used to be. I'm talking World War II. Clear cut, you know what I'm sayin'? America was

American, one hundred percent. To hell with all this modern crap. Tryin' to confuse everybody with Vietnam ten years too late. Send the boys to Central America. Let 'em prove what they're worth down there. Blow the fucking commies to kingdom come. Hell, we know it ain't pretty. We know what it costs to keep this country, to run this country. Fuck the rest of the world. Easy to be critical when it's not you that has to act. Easy to be critical when it's not you that's getting slaughtered. I'm talkin' us, you and me, buddy, our children and families, for god's sake."

Goo thought of the last time he'd seen his mother. She was in the hospital with her cancer.

"I knew you'd be here sooner or later," she said. "If it's for money, I ain't got any."

"I just wanted to tell you I was sorry," said Goo.

"Well, don't be. It's a hell of a relief, if you wanta know the truth. It's the medicine that's awful. Damn Medicaid don't cover the good stuff." She asked for her lipstick and a comb. "You seen Betty?"

"No."

"She's gone and put your son in a home, not that I blame her."

"I know. I've been to see him."

"And they let you in?"

"I don't go in. They bring 'em outside when the weather's good. You can see from the road."

Goo's mother started to cry. "I've tried to manage what was right, you know I have."

"I'm not your fault."

"Then whose, Goo?"

"Some say the war."

"Crap. Plenty of people go to war. Some just turn out better than others." She looked out the window. "My bed's wet. On your way out, tell the nurse."

Goo kissed her. She hugged him. She told him he smelled. She cried some more, then let him go.

In the hall, Goo passed a Hare Krishna. It was his brother, Roy. Roy took him down to the cafeteria, bought

93

him a cup of coffee, and told him all about his new spiritual life. "'Course Mom says it's what gave her cancer. Still screams every time I walk into the room."

Goo pulled at the sole strand of hair left on his brother's head. Back in high school they shared a room, slept in the same bed. Roy's hair was long then. It had a way of draping on Goo in the night. Roy left home for New York. He was supposed to be an actor, make it big, buy his own swimming pool.

Goo said to the old man, "Ever wonder when you'll land on the spot where you can no longer fool yourself, where you know for sure you're nothing, just like you always suspected, you're what you most often feared?"

"Hell," the man laughed. "You ain't even makin' sense."

■

Kate and Angus walked from the barn to the back door. Kate, with the gun, led the way. She looked at Codder sleeping and his ugly feet still sticking up. She positioned the pistol against the arch of his left, pulled the trigger, then shot the right.

Codder woke for an instant, saw Angus, the blood, then his wife, crazed and brandishing a gun. Kate snarled and shot him in the face. Just before he died he got a great view of her gums.

Kate told Angus, "Come on. We've got to get you across the state line."

"The state line?"

"Sure. It's all part of the plan."

"What plan? They won't suspect me."

"The hell they won't. You're my lover, aren't you?"

"You crazy bitch, I've got six kids!"

"Then come on!"

■

The old man turned off the freeway and went down a side road. "Gotta drop some wood off to my daughter." He asked Goo to unload. "'Bout half of what's there. Any-

94

where's fine. She can get her boy to restack it tomorrow."
He went over to the door and knocked. "Linda?"

It took a minute for a light to come on. "Dad? That you?"

"Who the hell you think it is?"

Wrapped in a bathrobe, she let him in. "Ain't you ever heard of a telephone?"

As Goo finished throwing the wood off the truck, the beam of a flashlight hit his face and a kid's voice said, "Who're you?"

"Get that goddamn light outta my face."

"Tell me who you are first."

"Get that goddamn light outta my face!"

"Why? You crazy or something?" The kid clicked it off.

"You oughta be in bed."

"I might oughta, but I ain't. Do me a favor, will ya? I caught me a lizard. Hold him for a minute." The kid clicked back on the light.

"I said, get that fucking light off me!"

"It's not on you. It's on my lizard. I wanta see what it does to his eyes."

"Your lizard ain't gonna have any eyes if you don't kill that light. I'll pull his fuckin' head off."

"You better not."

"Then kill the light!"

"No!"

Goo yanked at the lizard's head and pointed the blood spurting creature at the boy who immediately dropped the flashlight and screamed, "He's killed my lizard! He's killed my lizard!"

The daughter peered out. "Tommy, I told you to go to bed!"

"I caught me a lizard. That man pulled his head off!"

"Don't be ridiculous."

"Look at this blood!"

"Get in this house!"

■

95

"I can't believe we killed him, Angus. Just like that. Damn, what a feeling. And I'm not at all sorry. I'm happier now than I've been in my whole entire life." She pulled onto I-77, shifted into fourth, and squeezed her lover's crotch. "Yahoo!"

■

The old man took a pint out of the glove compartment. He took a swig then offered it to Goo. Goo handed it back empty. "What I offered you was a sip, not the whole goddamn thing," the man said. Goo took the lizard head out of his pocket and put it on his tongue. He chewed it with his mouth open. The old man pulled over. "I've had enough of you. Git the hell out." Goo pulled his knife, but the old man whacked him over the head with the empty bottle and pushed him out on the shoulder of the road before he could do anything with it.

■

Kate sped out of West Virginia. "The state line! The goddamn state line! We made it!"

"With murder it doesn't matter nothin' 'bout a state line."

"Damnit Angus, didn't you see *Bonnie and Clyde*?"

"Have you ever heard of extradition?"

"Extra-what?"

"Jesus! If I'd known you were this crazy, I'd never've agreed to help."

"But you did, baby. And didn't nobody force you."

■

Goo stumbled toward a Denny's. He made it to the to-go window and ordered a cup of coffee.

"Cream or sugar?" said the girl.

"Black."

She filled the cup, sealed on a top, put it in a bag with cream and sugar anyway, and stapled it shut. "That'll be forty-five cents." She noticed his head. "Hey, you OK? Need an extra napkin?"

■

Kate saw the Denny's sign and wanted a Coke. She sped into the parking lot and almost hit Goo. "Fucking asshole!" she screamed at him. "What are you trying to do? Get yourself fucking killed?"

She parked. "Want anything, Angus?" Angus didn't answer. She rapped her nails on the dashboard. They were at their perfect length and she admired them. She etched her name on the windshield, then smeared it out. "Well?" she said.

Still no answer.

Kate lit a cigarette. She took a deep drag and glanced in the rearview mirror. She saw Goo trying to hitch a ride. "Jesus," she said to herself, and still watching him, told Angus, "Get out of my car, honey."

"What?"

"You heard me. Get out."

"Why?"

"My plan, stupid."

"You can't just leave me here. How'm I supposed to get home?"

"You're a grown man, you'll think of something."

She leaned over and kissed him. He remembered why he loved her.

"And don't call me until after Codder's funeral," she said.

Kate pulled up to Goo. She leaned over, opened the passenger door, and said, "Where ya goin'?"

He bent down. "Outta this rain's good enough for me."

"Well come on then. Quick."

Kate drove back to Lavalette. She flicked through the radio stations. "Ever notice how you can't get anything decent when there's a storm on?"

Goo didn't say anything, he just watched the road, the white lines speeding by. When Kate pulled up to her house and the garage doors opened automatically, he said, "What's goin' on?"

"Just do as I tell you, baby, and you'll have the time of your life."

She led him into the kitchen. She poured him a drink. She put her hand on his crotch. She pulled his belt loose, unbuckled his pants, then unzipped his fly. She got down on her knees and took him in her mouth. The taste of him made her want to gag, but she kept at him. She worked his pants down around his ankles. "Step out of these for me."

She giggled at the sight of him, helpless, and with half a hard-on.

"Gimme my fuckin' pants back," he said.

She ran down the hall, knocking over plants and knick-knacks on her way. She let him catch her in the bedroom and pin her to the bed.

She kissed him. His breath was disgusting, but she kissed him for all she was worth. "Spit on me," she said. "I dare you to. Spit on me, you bastard." She slapped him. "You wanta fuck?" She slapped him again. "Then rip my clothes off me. I'm in a coma, see? I dare you. Go ahead, tear me to shreds."

He ripped open her shirt, then her pants. He buried his head between her legs.

"Sentimental creep!" She pushed him away. "I'm gonna put in my diaphragm. Go back in the kitchen and wait."

Kate listened as he walked down the hall. She picked up the phone and called the police.

Goo stood in the kitchen. He cried. He opened Kate's purse and found the gun. He heard her coming down the hall and dropped it in his coat pocket.

She was naked. "OK," she said, "let's go. Show me what you can do. I like it from behind, like a dog, see?" She got Goo hard enough to penetrate her. "Make me feel something you son of a bitch, make me feel something!"

She pulled away as soon as he came. His semen ran down her legs. She wiped it and laughed. Goo grabbed her by the shoulders. "What is it you want from me? What is it you want?"

She reached for her purse. She didn't find what she was looking for. She quickly scanned the counter, then saw Goo's hand go into his pocket. Her back prickled. "What are you doing with that? It's mine. Give it back."

"No way, lady. I've worked too hard for this." He cocked and uncocked the gun, cocked it again, caressed it. "Success," he whispered, a weird smile on his face. He locked eyes with Kate, put the gun in his mouth, and pulled the trigger.

Kate didn't blink. She watched him fall. A rush went through her like pure absolution. Success is how much you can get away with.

THE END OF
THE SEASON

WELL, ANOTHER SUMMER'S PRACTICALLY GONE AND I haven't written a word. I'm a lazy pig. I admit it. Here it is the eve of our last day. Won't you please meet Cheezy and Jo, the goodtime gals who own the place. They're hard drinking lesbians of the old school. It's their first summer in the tourist trade. How'd they get here? Won Lotto. Used the money to finance their dream: land-owning. Found it plenty cheap and pretty right here in Loon Lake, Saskatchewan. And it ain't got a speck to do with that novel by Doctorow.

Cheezy and Jo hired some locals to help 'em build the cabins. They only completed five. The locals were appalled when they saw the color scheme, and ran off. Who in their right mind painted lake houses sixteen thousand fluorescent shades? But Cheezy and Jo got a deal on some indoor/outdoor Day-Glo and figured what the hell. The Saskatchewanese traditionally welcome strangers with arms wide open. About Cheezy and Jo they're beginning to wonder.

The biggest cabin's only eight foot by ten. The idea is

to encourage the guests to spend time outdoors. After all, that's what we're here for.

Cheezy and Jo are from Toronto which explains their love of weather, as Toronto doesn't have any. Not so at Loon Lake. For the seven weeks of summer, it's paradise. My suntan's great. Problems are few. And though I wouldn't turn down a massage, I'm pretty relaxed.

"Ya-hoo," hoots Cheezy, chugging a beer.

"Right-o," says Jo, spitting out a cigar tip. They laugh like crazy 'cause Kruschev's out paddling around in his inner tube, swigging a bottle of vodka, and doing tongue tricks.

Out of Cabin Two peeks a dark beauty. Vita Vail. That's not her real name. I've changed it to protect her. She's a famous novelist who's come here to work. Like me, she hasn't written a word, and she's very moody about it.

When Vita first saw Cabin Two she had a fit. Said, "Hell, my limo's bigger than this!"

Jo rubbed her five o'clock shadow. "Listen, Princess, we put in a goddamn loft so we could squeeze you in a desk. I wouldn't complain if I were you."

Now Vita's having another fit. She stomps her feet and hollers at the swimming crowd, "Shut up out there! I'm trying to fucking think!" She storms over to Cheezy and Jo. "I want you to know this place is about as peaceful as a yeast infection."

A million years ago, before the first successful novel, Vita and Jo were lovers.

"I need some ice," Vita demands. "I might as well be as drunk as the rest of you!"

"Max?! We'll have Max bring you some."

Vita opens her change purse.

"No tipping," winks Cheezy.

■

Kruschev, still paddling around, is, as you might have speculated, the ex-head of the Soviet Union. Not nearly as dead as everyone thinks. He's been hiding in Western

Canada disguised as a retired Ukrainian railway worker. When he's not in his inner tube, he's in his chauffeur-driven Volkswagen. He's so fat Cheezy's had to remove the front seat. Max just plops him into the back like a three-hundred-pound pillow. Kruschev visits the Ukrainian community daily. Last Christmas he dressed up as Santa Claus and threw candy.

Kruschev paddles over to Vita Vail who's walking the perimeters of the lake with her second scotch. Kruschev says the first English word that comes to mind, "Disneyland."

I watch from my cabin where my summer boyfriend, who ought to be working on his father's farm, is massaging me. Miss Finny from Cabin Four has brought us a piece of Tunnel of Fudge. We've rubbed it all over ourselves in honor of Finny who's done nothing his whole vacation but bake, bake, bake.

Boyfriend and I met at the Liquor Board Store. He used to work there Tuesdays and Thursdays until I rescued him. I'm the first person he's ever known from the South. I come up here to escape the humidity.

Jo says to Cheezy, "Take Vita another drink."

"You take her one. I'm not her goddamn slave." Cheezy remembers all too well what a pain in the ass that loft was. "We oughta be chargin' her double. Nobody appreciates what you do for 'em."

"I do."

"I'd kill ya if you didn't."

"Like hell."

"Like hell my ass."

Cheezy gooses Jo.

"Stop that."

"Can't help it, honey. Every time I look at you I just get so hungry."

"The meat loaf'll be ready in an hour."

"That mean we got time for a 'Charlie's Angels' re-run?"

"Fucking A."

"E-e-e-e," squeals Cheezy, carrying Jo down the

porch. Jo's the size of a filing cabinet and Cheezy can barely lift her. Still they sing, "Two little pigs, fingers in their figs."

Cheezy and Jo write rhymes. This is their latest.

■

Kruschev holds a round table discussion on The Problems of the World. Under the table boyfriend extends his leg into my crotch.

Kruschev blames the Americans for everything. The Canadians, with the exception of Boyfriend, agree whole-heartedly. This means I'll have to either wash the dinner dishes or answer for the sins of my country. I choose the dishes.

Miss Finny asks to be excused and returns to his cabin to work on something "very special." Miss Finny's body is covered in bristly red hair. Every day he experiments with different colored clothing. Today is fuschia. He resembles a rusty azalea bush.

Jo's hair's a mess. Frizzy and long. Cheezy brushes it, pulls it back, ties it up in a silk polka-dot necktie that used to belong to her daddy (before he was killed in World War II). Cheezy never knew him, but she sure knows this tie. She wore it when she was a little girl on several Halloweens. She wore it again when she joined the Alice B. Toklas Society at McGill. And she wore it when *Annie Hall* came out.

Jo's hand reaches up and squeezes Cheezy's. They look out at the lake like they're the luckiest two people alive.

■

Vita sits for an hour with a pencil in her mouth, staring at a blank page. She has not yet discovered what she's writing about. She realizes, of course, that a draft or so later she'll pull out her Olivetti portable and type it up, edit it, then type it up again. The day will even come when she'll sit down to her computer and put it onto disk. She tries to see the book in finished form. See herself signing copies at the launch. See herself afterwards, in bed, eating a box of peanut brittle and reading it.

She's been advanced twice the usual amount on the sure-to-be-smash. A Vita Vail Romp, to quote her salivating agent. She'd like to decapitate that bastard. Poke out his eyes and use his head as a bowling ball. Strike.

She looks out at the lake. Wishes Cheezy and Jo had a ski boat. Writes something finally about a girl who sees imaginary wires out of some skyscraper in Chicago. The girl thinks she's some kind of psychic trapeze artist and jumps out the window. She ends up in the hospital, bandaged from head to toe, and berates her lover, "Why didn't you stop me?!"

Vita goes for a walk. Masturbates in the bush. She cries. She tells herself you can't have everything. She wonders if it was wrong to break things off with Mary Ann.

She sees herself chopped into pot roast-sized pieces, wrapped in cellophane, marked down and spoiling on some supermarket shelf.

She walks to the end of Loon Lake Road to use the pay phone. She calls her analyst. They hold their usual session, long distance.

■

Boyfriend tells me, "Next year I'll go to agricultural school. Then in two more, I'll take over the farm. But I'll raise cattle, not grain. I plan to make a living." He pokes me with a finger.

I step on his toes, give him a kiss. He licks my lips, says, "At some point I'll have to get married." Licks 'em again. "Have to to have kids. But you can come visit." He squeezes my butt. "We'll take 'em hunting. Teach 'em how to curl, play hockey."

"I don't know how to play hockey."

"Can you ice skate?"

"Sure."

"Then there's nothing to it."

He watches me button my shirt and says, "Sometimes I think about joining the Marines. God, I'd love to travel.

Ever been to South Dakota?"

Boyfriend's eyes make me crazy. They go on forever. Blue like the sky out here.

We hitch out to his father's fields and fuck. Have to wear a lot of Off but it's worth it. He's sexy as all get out. Has chunky lips, just like the rest of him. One big cuddly sausage.

■

Kruschev is forming a marching band. So far he's the only member. He wanted to be drum major, however his talent on the saxophone placed him elsewhere. Max, the chauffeur, found him a green and gold band uniform at the Sally Ann. It was much too small so Jo cut it in half and stapled it onto Kruschev's regular clothes. Kruschev marches around the lake playing "Gimme a Pigfoot and a Bottle of Beer." It makes me homesick. What I wouldn't give for a good, Southern dinner.

■

Vita Vail bangs her fists against her head. God, am I glad I'm not famous like her and am just here on vacation.

■

The meat loaf is moose. Kruschev is extremely excited about the menu and will feed very little to his dog. Vita just picks. Mainly she drinks. Boyfriend is starved. So am I. Miss Finny fusses with a special cake that is an exact replica of Cheezy and Jo's cottage. Tears of pride swell in his eyes as he sets it onto the table. It's painful for him to cut it. Kruschev pinches him as he reaches over to hand me my piece. Kruschev doesn't realize Miss Finny's a man.

"Staying busy's the secret to success," says Finny. He owns two houses, a car, and a large parcel of Saskatchewan farmland which he resents because it was given to him by his father. Miss Finny is from a family he'd rather forget.

Cheezy and Jo get all choked up making a speech

about how great the summer's been and how we've each helped to make it the best time of their life. They say they'd invite us all back next summer free of charge if they could afford to, but business is business. They pass around their guest book for us to sign.

"My autograph must be worth a fortune," says Kruschev writing vigorously. "Much more valuable than my paintings." I forgot to mention Kruschev's considerable talent with the brushes. I've bought two of his pictures. One of Caroline Kennedy and one of an unknown woman searching an unknown soldiers' cemetery for her son.

Boyfriend's taking me to the Meadow Lake Stampede. I ask Kruschev, "Can Max drive us?"

"Sure." Kruschev puts butter on his toes and lets his dog lick it off.

■

On the drive to the Stampede, Max speaks. He says his father used to be an ambassador to China. Max is fluent in Mandarin and has a doctoral degree in Chinese puppetry. "Fat lot of good it did me, eh?, driving around some has-been politician."

The Stampede is a bit of a bore. Dusty and hot, but the sunset is spectacular and makes all the waiting around worth it. Plus the cowboys. Then come the mosquitoes.

I tell Boyfriend how Saskatchewan reminds me of Texas. He's impatient. Sees some of his friends and goes off to say hi.

When he hasn't come back in half an hour, I go looking for him. He acts like he doesn't even know me when I find him. He always does this when we're in public so no one'll know he's gay. Usually it doesn't faze me. Tonight it hurts. In fact, I've had it. I decide to go back to Loon Lake without him. Should have never fooled with him to begin with. Serves me right.

Vita Vail is on the fairgrounds. I catch up with her. She's unusually friendly. We have some laughs, talk about New York, and smoke a joint she has. I think maybe she'll take a real liking to me and help me out with my career.

When she asks what I do, I tell her I'm a writer. I say it with pride.

"Have you published?"

"Short stories and one book, small press stuff."

"Well take it from me, you'll never be happier. I've written five best sellers, all of 'em shit except the first. I'm changing all that now, though. Gonna write me a novel about a woman who turns into a pot roast." She looks off into the vast distance.

"Listen," I say, wringing my hands. "Could I ask you a favor? Could you possibly introduce me to your agent? I've tried like a dog to get one, and they're all very nice and friendly and usually read a story or two, but they tell me I won't sell. But I'd sell if they wanted me to. It's just a matter of getting the right person interested, isn't it?"

Vita sympathizes with my dilemma but I can tell it depresses her. She wants to go back to camp which is not such a bad idea.

I run into Boyfriend who's waiting by the car with Max. I ignore him completely and instruct Max not to unlock Boyfriend's door. Boyfriend tells me to go to hell and kicks in the fender. I feel like a real bastard but tell myself I'll have to start living without him tomorrow so I might as well start practicing tonight.

The sky's perfectly clear. I roll my window down humming "Better Luck Next Time."

■

Cheezy and Jo lure me into a midnight game of water chicken. Cheezy's on Jo. I'm on Kruschev. Vita's on Miss Finny. I miss Boyfriend.

Kruschev and I win. He loves winning. Wants to chicken fight Reagan or Connie Stevens, he says.

Cheezy slips her bathing suit off under water and puts it over her head. She attacks Jo with a mud ball. Pretty soon they look like a feature out of *National Geographic*.

Finny brings out a raspberry cheesecake. I go back with Vita to Cabin Two. She hands me back the story I gave her to read.

"Not bad," she says, taking off her glasses. "Though I can see why someone would say there's not much of a market, but we'll talk."

"OK talk."

"Tomorrow."

■

Boyfriend's sitting on the steps to my cabin. I'm so damn glad to see him and relieved and in love that I feel like a greeting card, all flowers and slow motion. We kiss and cuddle and my hands go through his hair and he leans against my shoulder and says, "Don't go. Don't leave me. Ever."

■

Cheezy fixes a night cap for her and Jo. Takes them with her to bed.

Jo's sad. Cheezy can tell. "What's wrong?"

"Just feel empty's all." Jo sips the thick liquid and rolls over.

"Menopause," Cheezy tells her.

"Lesbians are exempt from menopause."

"No they're not."

"Well they oughta be."

■

Miss Finny reads the newspaper. Brushes his teeth. He climbs into bed without messing up the covers. He recites a mantra he learned fifteen years ago that makes you forget about desire, sex, and loneliness so you can get to sleep and dream about them instead.

■

Boyfriend makes a hell of a lot of noise coming, sounds like a gorilla. Cheezy and Jo, on the other hand, sound like cats. Boyfriend takes twenty dollars out of my wallet. Says, "To remember you by." I love parting with money.

■

After breakfast Vita asks me back over to Cabin Two. It's rainy and chilly and she's got a fire going.

"Talked to my agent early this morning. He said to send him some stuff. I'll leave you the address." She lights a cigarette. "Now, if you'll excuse me, I have to pack."

■

Happy as a clam, I take Kruschev's inner tube out on the lake. I get drenched dreaming of success, fame, and the lecture circuit.

How jealous all my friends'll be!

■

Back at the cabin Boyfriend's dancing to Bowie. I put on "Hello, Dolly" and belt it out with good ol' Carol Channing.

Miss Finny, from his cabin, sings along while icing a last batch of muffins. Cheezy comes round to say, "I'm inviting all the guests for one last lunch. RSVP."

■

Kruschev carves the roast. It smells like heaven. Max looks suspicious. Vita turns green. She says she's decided to become a vegetarian. Jo gives her an avocado and a cantaloupe. Vita runs from the table retching.

Cheezy and Jo settle in front of the TV. The Toronto Blue Jays are up against the New York Yankees. Cheezy and Jo wear Blue Jay T-shirts and sun visors. They sing along with "O Canada" then bite the caps off a couple of beers.

The Yankees make three runs in the first inning. The Blue Jays strike out. By the end of the third it's seven to nothing. Jo's worried. Cheezy goes to the kitchen and returns with an uncooked chicken. She puts it in a jock strap, sets it on top of the TV, and surrounds it with four quarters, tails up.

"Germ warfare," says Kruschev. The Blue Jays get a hit.

■

I meander over to Vita's only to find she's gone. Vacated on the sly! All her bags. Everything! She hasn't left me the address of her agent. She hasn't even paid her bill!

I feel furiously desperate for about five minutes, then I spot a notebook on the edge of the loft. It's Vita's journal. I contemplate phoning *People* magazine with the scoop, but realize Vita's not that famous. I read it instead. There's nothing remarkable: sexual fantasies, personal frustrations, professional anxieties, musings about life, Mary Ann's phone number at her parents. The most recent entry is only one line, scratched out, "We miss only the dead, only that which we cannot have."

On the way back to Cheezy and Jo's I throw the journal into the lake. Let 'em find it in years to come. Then I realize it was written in felt tip.

■

Boyfriend and I sit on the porch. We watch Miss Finny pack his car. Listen to Cheezy and Jo whoop it up as the Blue Jays get closer to victory.

Kruschev walks by carrying a miniature Canadian flag. He's decided to reenter the political arena via the mayor's race in Saskatoon. Do we have any ideas for a speech?

Boyfriend rests his knee against mine. Smiles. Looks at the lake and beyond.

I laugh 'cause I don't know what else to do. Getting older and older, and still not knowing.

ABOUT THE AUTHOR

Peter McGehee is the author of the novel *Boys Like Us* (St. Martin's and HarperCollins) and the story collection *Beyond Happiness* (Stubblejumper Press) which he also performed as a one-person play across Canada, in New York, and in San Francisco. He wrote the songs for and performed in the musical revues *The Quinlan Sisters* and *The Fabulous Sirs*, both of which toured extensively.

Originally from Arkansas, he moved to Canada in the early eighties—to Saskatoon. Currently, he resides in Toronto.

ABOUT THE ILLUSTRATOR

Dik Campbell was born in St. John's, Newfoundland and now lives in Saskatoon. His most recent exhibition was "Pressing" about media misrepresentation of gays. Dik is the Production Manager and Art Director of *NeWest Review* and Program Co-ordinator at AKA Gallery.